# TERROR ZONE

# TERROR ZONE

## Vince Rogers

BRAY MINE
PUBLISHING

Cover by Casey Booth
CaseyBooth.me

Edited by James Powell
TheFictionCoach.com

ISBN: 979-8-9918265-2-5 (Hardback)
ISBN: 979-8-9918265-1-8 (Paperback)
ISBN: 979-8-9918265-0-1 (eBook)

First Edition 2024

To my friends,

old and new,

thanks for

the adventures

and camaraderie.

# TERROR ZONE

# ONE

"I don't care, as long as there's blood."

Caleb stood looking over Gabe's shoulder at the laptop screen and the list of movies displayed there.

"Don't worry, we can download anything, and not just movies," Gabe said adjusting his backward Raiders hat, which tamed a long jungle of thick black hair. He leaned forward in his chair and pointed at the list of categories. "Look, there's movies, music, games, software, porn, anime...anything. What'd I tell you? Pirating movies is killer!"

Evan watched as Caleb's mouth drew up into a grin. Across the bar, to Evan's right, James leaned back in his chair and smiled under his St. Louis Cardinals cap. He fumbled a baseball between his hands and tossed it up in the air to himself. His red Ozark

Junior High Baseball t-shirt clung tight to his athletic frame.

"Sick!" Logan said with a smirk to Evan's left. He adjusted the collar on his green short sleeved button-up and put a foot on his chair's footrest. With his high, slicked back blond hair he looked like a California kid, though he'd probably never been outside Missouri in his life.

Evan sat uneasily between Logan and James. His wide eyes held a look of anxiety and nerves behind his thick-rimmed glasses. His hands pulled at the bottom of his blue polo shirt, which felt too short for him.

He looked away, studying the room to distract himself. It was the first time he'd been in Caleb's basement, and it was amazing how large it was. He figured it was big, considering the size of the rest of the house, but big enough for a furnished theater and full bar filled with dozens of fancy liquor bottles? Evan wasn't prepared for that. He wondered what else was in store.

Down the bar counter where they sat, a stack of Domino's boxes called his name and made his stomach rumble. Evan took a sip of his Coke. Looking around the counter, he realized he was the only one who put his can on a coaster.

"This is going to be awesome," Caleb said. "As long as it doesn't give our Wi-Fi a virus. My dad'll get pissed. He almost didn't let us use the basement while gone for the weekend!"

"Pfft." Gabe rolled his eyes and crossed his arms over his black Exodus t-shirt. "I'd hate to piss off Uncle Moneybags. Don't worry, this is completely safe. My brother's done it tons of times."

"Let's find a movie," James said. He tossed his baseball to Logan over Evan's head. "And it had better be scary."

Evan gulped and put his hands in his lap.

Logan leaned back and tossed the ball to himself, kicking the seat of Evan's chair.

"Let's check out the porn page," Logan suggested, touching his hair to make sure it hadn't fallen out of place. Evan assumed it was more of a nervous tick than Logan thinking his slicked-back golden locks were out of place.

"We're not watching porn," Caleb sighed, shaking his head. "We're doing a scary movie."

Logan shrugged and tossed the ball over Evan again, making him flinch. James caught it and rolled it between his hands.

"I'm still surprised as hell Evan came tonight," James said. "When he wasn't on the bus, I thought for sure he'd wuss out."

"I told you, I couldn't ride the bus. My mom didn't sign the form," Evan admitted, instantly regretting opening his mouth. He pushed his glasses up from the tip of his nose. He felt his cheeks flush.

"Momma's boy!"

James tossed the ball back to Logan as if it were the talking totem for making fun of Evan. Whoever had the ball had permission to hurl the next insult.

"Yeah! Momma's boy!" Logan said. "You're like Jason Voorhees, but instead of slashing people to bits, you just suck."

"Shut up!" Evan shot back. He folded his arms across his chest in a frustrated pout.

Caleb shook his head at the pair and turned his attention back to the screen. "You're sure this is safe?" he said, nudging Gabe's shoulder. "I don't want to get caught doing anything illegal."

Gabe looked back over his shoulder at him. "Look, like I said, my brother did this all the time. He never got in trouble. At least, not for this."

Evan finally lashed out and swiped at the ball as it flew over his head. He missed by a mile and his chair wobbled in large pendulum-like stomps that echoed on the tile floor. Impulsively, he shouted "Shit dick!" as he slapped his hands on the bar to steady himself. The boys around him laughed, and his face turned as red as his Coke can.

"Just for the record," he said, "I wasn't the only one who didn't ride the bus."

Gabe held up his hands and said, "Hey, don't bring me into this. I drove here. Plus, I'm the oldest and I'm getting you little shits free movies, so I get a pass."

"Well, he gets a pass as long it's scary," Logan said. He examined the ball and then added, "Scary and sexy. I'd better see at least one nipple tonight."

"No porn!" Gabe said, slamming a hand on the counter. He shook his head and returned his eyes to the laptop. "But don't worry, we'll get a *really* scary one tonight."

Evan gulped as he stared at the back of Gabe's laptop where he saw a collage of heavy metal and horror movie stickers. They made him as unsettled as imagining the movie they'd watch. This was the first time being invited to movie night and he didn't want to blow it. He had to prove he belonged.

"You guys always watch scary movies?" Evan asked, staring at a sticker on the laptop of a skeleton climbing out of a bleeding body. MEGA-DETH was scrawled over top.

"Well," Gabe shrugged, "it depends on what you consider scary."

*The stickers on your laptop,* Evan thought.

Before he could respond, James caught the talking totem and said, "Let's see, thunderstorms, the dark, his own shadow…"

"Don't forget girls!" Logan blurted out.

Evan turned to Logan, puffing up his chest. "Shut it!" he said. "You pecker mouth!"

Gabe snickered from behind his screen and then lowered his head. Caleb put his hand to his forehead while James winced and let out a "Jesus, Evan!"

"Evan, stop cussing," Logan shook his head. "You sound super homo."

Without thinking, Evan replied, "Eat my dick!"

The guys laughed while Evan sat there fuming.

"Are we going to pick out a movie or what?" Gabe asked, forcing the laughter to die down. "Anything we pick might take a while to download. Let's get started before the pizza gets cold."

Down the counter, the tower of Domino's pizza boxes sat in a bright dome from a can light. The smell wafted down and made Evan's stomach grumble again. For a moment, he'd entirely forgotten the impending horror movie and harbored excitement toward dinner and a show.

"Did Rachel order plain cheese?" he asked.

Logan caught the ball again.

"Evan," he said, "you sound like that kid from *Home Alone* that got molested."

He tossed the ball back to James.

"Funny, I don't remember *that* being in the movie."

"Will you guys quit fucking around and help us pick a movie?"

Caleb's face reddened with irritation while Evan's blushed from embarrassment. Evan would have been glad to see his friend standing up for him, if he didn't know it had more to do with saving movie night than protecting his honor. Still, Evan relaxed his tense shoulders knowing that he was pushing for the teasing to stop.

"Sorry, C," James said. He sat the ball on the counter and leaned around the laptop with Logan. Evan moved to look over the top of the screen. Gabe shook his head and simply turned the laptop on the counter where all the boys could see.

Each movie on the website was represented by its movie poster. Gabe scrolled slowly down the page, giving Evan a good look. His stomach clenched. What he saw was far worse than the stickers.

"How about that one?" Logan pointed to a poster with scantily clad girls staring up at a killer wielding a large drill with a long, sharp bit. It was titled *The Slumber Party Massacre,* and the obvious sleepover sex appeal made Evan want it stricken from the list. God knew what the killer did with the drill. Not to mention, the suggestion of lewd women made him blush just thinking about it.

"Let's keep looking," he said quickly.

"You scared of seeing naked chicks, Evan?" Logan said, rolling his eyes.

"No! I just," Evan slouched and rubbed his hands together, "you know, I want something that's *really* out there."

Gabe looked at him with a smirk. "Hear that, Logan? Evan's pushing the envelope more than you."

"Well, shit!" Logan folded his arms and mimicked Evan's earlier pouting efforts. "Maybe *he* should pick the movie then."

"Actually," Caleb cocked his head, "that's not a bad idea."

James and Logan looked at each other, their eyebrows scrunched and their mouths agape.

"Are you kidding?" James raised his hands like a coach to a ref making a bad call.

"There's no way he picks a good one," Logan shook his head. "This is his first movie night. He doesn't know what we like. I told you not to invite him."

Evan's eyes shot over to Caleb.

"I thought you said everyone wanted me to come," Evan said.

— 9 —

"I wanted to make sure you'd show up," Caleb admitted. "Gabe thought it was cool if you came over."

"That's not true. I said I didn't care." Gabe frowned, then turned to Evan. "I only met you the one time, at Caleb's fourteenth birthday last year. Honestly, I thought you were annoying."

Evan slumped back in his chair and folded his arms. He fought hard to keep back the tears. Trying to belong with the guys seemed like an idea doomed from the start. He'd never be as funny as James or Logan, never cool or rich enough to be like Caleb. He sure as hell couldn't grow enough facial hair or become fifteen overnight to match Gabe.

He never stood a chance.

"How about you pick the movie," Gabe said. "Just make it something from the horror section. It could be *The Ghost of Frankenstein* for all I care."

"I care!" James shouted. Then he looked Evan in the eye. "Don't pick that atrocity."

"Don't listen to those idiots," Caleb said, leaning across the bar to Evan. "Pick whatever you want. I'm sorry I didn't prepare you for these bullies."

"We have the same classes!" Logan said. "He knows what we're like. We do this to everybody. We don't mean anything by it."

"I'm not in the same classes," Gabe said, smirking. He cupped his hands behind his head and leaned back. "Not even the same school!"

"Yeah, but you're in the same grade, right?" Logan jumped back. "Fifteen and still in the eighth grade. I thought people from *Clever* were supposed to be *clever!*"

Gabe pushed his chair back. His eyes narrowed, ready for murder, but before he could reply, Caleb put a hand on his shoulder. They exchanged a knowing look and Gabe sat back down.

"What do you say?" Caleb asked, turning back to Evan. "See anything you like?"

The first poster was for *The Evil Dead*. Just the title made him squirm, so that was out. Many on the first page were from the *Friday the 13th* series, which had a mainstream reputation as a slasher, so that wouldn't do. The boys mentioned *Aliens*, *Pet Sematary*, *Hellraiser*, and *My Bloody Valentine*, but Evan's ears went numb, and their shouted suggestions all sounded muffled.

Gabe clicked to the next page. More and more titles went by, each more frightening than the last, all with ominous names and posters. *Sleepaway Camp*, *The Prowler*, and *Cannibal Holocaust* especially got his attention. What nightmares! All the posters were collages of vicious killers, half-naked women, and the promise of blood by the bucket. The more he saw, the more the posters looked the same.

Around them, the basement was still and quiet. Only the gentle hum of the minifridge and the taps of Gabe's fingers on the laptop sounded in the large space. Caleb's parents were out of town and his sister was at a friend's house. Evan was eerily aware of the world around them at the bar, how empty it was, and how far away grownups were. It made him uneasy. He could feel his heart thumping in his throat. The smell of Domino's pizza combined with the cloying smell from Logan's hair gel made his stomach queasy.

He shivered in his chair with his eyes glazing over as Gabe gently scrolled further. Evan sensed James and Logan paying greater attention to him, so he kept his attention on the screen. They made it to page three and Evan felt no better with the titles and posters. If anything, they were getting worse. The guys groaned and sighed around him. Soon, he would have to pick a movie like some poor dungeon victim choosing his torturer's weapon.

Finally, as Gabe clicked to page four, Evan raised a hand, extended a finger, and pointed to the screen.

"There! That one," he said, closing his eyes as everyone's attention drew to the screen.

"Damn," he heard Gabe say. "That looks sick!"

"Poster looks like it was from the fifties," James said with skepticism in his voice. "Are you sure you want to watch *that* one?"

Evan opened his eyes to see his finger aiming at a poster for a movie called *Terror Zone*. "The portal opened and out stepped THE BEING FROM…TERROR ZONE!" the black-and-white poster screamed at them. "HORROR UNIMAGINABLE! DO NOT WATCH! BEWARE THE BEING!"

The warnings seemed lost on the guys, but they petrified Evan. He could only stare behind his glasses with wide eyes at the center of the poster where a glowing skull screamed over the scorched earth below it.

"Yeah," Evan said with a gulp. "It looks scary…might be good."

"Good pick, Evan!" Caleb went over and put a hand on Evan's shoulder.

Gabe turned the laptop around to himself and clicked to start the download. Evan zipped his lip, conflicted between protesting and not wanting to look like a pansy.

"Never heard of it," James said with a frown.

"Maybe it'll be stupid gory and we'll see some blood," Logan said, fixing his hair with his fingers. "Or maybe some boobs."

"Keep it in your pants," Caleb said with a smirk. "How long will it take to download?"

Gabe shrugged as he clicked around. "It's weird," he said. "It looks like a smallish file, but it's going slow. Says it'll be twenty minutes, but I'm guessing ten or fifteen max."

"Long enough for a quick round of Call of Duty?" Logan asked.

"Yeah!" James said, hopping out of his chair. "Let's get one going while we wait."

Caleb led James and Logan away from the bar to the theater area at the opposite end of the basement. The room was a large rectangle with a sports bar on one end, a retro-styled movie theater on the other, and stairs leading to the main floor about halfway between them. Classic movie posters hung on the walls, illuminated by spotlights — *Back to the Future*, *Jaws*, *Conan the Destroyer*, *The Matrix* — along with a life-sized cutout of Sylvester Stallone as Rocky standing in the corner.

A wheeled popcorn cart straight out of a creepy Ray Bradbury carnival stood opposite the stairs in the middle with a large bag of kernels and a jug of oil on the lower shelf. Baseball and football memorabilia littered the shelves behind the bar, including an official and very used Kansas City Chiefs helmet that sat on a shelf above the bar with framed Chiefs jerseys below it.

Evan watched James and Logan climb into the plush leather recliners in the front row of the theater area. Caleb went through flipping on lights, then grabbed a remote from the tall wooden cabinet beside the large projector screen and turned on the high-mounted overhead projector. The screen took up almost the whole basement wall. Speakers behind the screen and beneath the risers chimed and swooshed as the Xbox splash screen flew into view.

Normally, Evan would have loved to play video games, but he clutched his hands, unable to move. Gabe pulled out his laptop charger and began to untangle the cable. Evan stared as if he were wrangling a snake in front of him.

His mind was on *Terror Zone*.

"What's the problem?" Gabe asked, not looking up from the cable.

"Nothing," Evan replied. "I don't have a problem. I was just thinking about playing Fortnite instead. I brought my Nintendo Switch and—"

"No, something's bugging you," Gabe said. He plugged the charger into the wall behind the bar and then into his laptop. The screen became noticeably brighter. "They're gone now, and I'm not going to razz you...not too much, at least. So enough with the Fortnite bullshit. Have you ever even seen a scary movie?"

Evan blinked and locked eyes with Gabe. Suddenly the bar seemed more like an interrogation table and Gabe a hardboiled detective.

"Of course I have," he said with a shrug. "Why do you think Caleb invited me?"

"That's not what Caleb told me." Gabe folded his arms and gave Evan the side eye. "Which movie's scarier: *The Exorcist* or *Poltergeist*?"

Evan's eyes searched around the room for an answer before he coughed one out.

"*Poltergeist*," he said. Then he added, "because it's got more blood?"

Gabe shook his head and frowned. "You're such a liar. You've never watched a scary movie in your life, have you?"

Evan's eyes dropped to the counter. "My parents won't let me watch them."

"They let you play Call of Duty, but they won't let you watch a horror movie?"

Evan continued looking at the floor.

"Hey, man, so what?" Gabe reached across and hit Evan's shoulder. "You do everything your parents tell you to do?"

"Well, I—"

"Doesn't matter! I don't see any parents around tonight." Gabe swept a palm around the room, showcasing the emptiness. "Hell, Rachel's not even here. Since I'm the oldest, I say I'm in charge. And I say whatever your parents say is bullshit. We do what we want tonight. What do you say?"

Evan shrugged. "It's not that," he said, glancing up at Gabe.

"What are you, chicken shit?"

Evan lowered his gaze again.

"Oh, shit," Gabe chuckled, "you are!"

"Don't tell the other guys," Evan looked over his shoulder. "Especially Caleb. I want him to like me."

Gabe narrowed his eyes and took a step back.

"You're not some poof, are you?"

"No," Evan said, waving his hands. "No, no! Nothing like that."

He looked over his shoulder again, then leaned over the bar as if confessing a murder to a bartender.

"I let Caleb cheat off me in Mr. Fox's class," he said. "I think he invited me to say thanks, but I don't want to just be friends because of that. I want him to think I'm cool, too, you know? Not just some kid who lets him cheat off his papers."

"Sorry to tell you," Gabe said, "but I don't think he'll think you're cool. No matter how much he cheats off you in Mr. Fuck's class."

"Fox," Evan corrected.

"I'd start by not letting him think you're scared. Caleb loves horror movies, almost as much as I do."

"I don't know how to do that!" Evan's voice was rising. He looked over his shoulder, saw the guys were still setting up the Call of Duty match, and turned back to Gabe. "It's my first scary movie. How do I keep from getting scared?"

Gabe sighed, then bit his lip. His mannerisms reminded Evan of Caleb, and he could easily see how the cousins were alike.

"When I was a kid," Gabe said, uncrossing his arms, "my older brother and I would ride roller coasters. He'd push me to ride bigger and bigger coasters. Sometimes he'd tease me when I was scared, but he bought me candy with his own money when I finally rode Wildfire at Silver Dollar City.

"He always told me it was okay if I shut my eyes, just so long as I didn't scream and try to jump off. I think it's the same with you. Doesn't matter how scared you get. Just shut your eyes and ride it out."

"Just shut my eyes," Evan repeated. "Think they'll notice I'm scared if I do that?"

"Oh, they will," Gabe said. "But if the movie's good enough, they won't care what you're doing. Especially during the scary bits."

Evan thought for a moment, then nodded.

"Alright," he said. "I'll try it."

"Great!" Gabe rolled his eyes. "I was *so* worried."

He gave Evan a hit on the arm and then moved to the pizza boxes.

On the laptop screen, Evan watched the download clock count down. Eleven minutes until showtime.

# TWO

"It's done!" Gabe called from the bar.

The guys were well into their round of Call of Duty and second slice of pizza, but Evan had hardly forgotten how scared he was about the movie. Caleb ran out of the theater room, flipping on the lights as he left.

"I'd love to swing one of those bats," James said from the front row of leather seats. He nodded toward the bar where framed St. Louis Cardinals jerseys hung above two signed wooden bats and multiple signed baseballs. "Even just once. I want to see how a major league bat whooshes through the air."

"I'd love to beat the shit out of Rocky," Logan said, gesturing toward the Rocky standee with his phone and then shadowboxing in his seat. His fists reached out toward the boxer's cutout. "You know, give ol' Sylvester another speech impediment."

James leaned over Logan's shoulder.

"Who are you texting? Jamie? Heather?"

Logan shook his head. "Better! Brooke from Biology. I love studying her anatomy."

"He probably just sends girls the eggplant emoji," Caleb said as he entered the room with Gabe.

"Isn't it catfishing," Gabe asked, "when you promise an eggplant but deliver a baby carrot?"

Evan snickered to himself in the back row, then aloud when he heard Caleb and James join in. It was Logan's turn for his face to turn red.

"Damn!" James said through his laughs. "That was a clean burn."

Caleb threw a thumb over his shoulder. "Hey, Logan. There's some burn cream in the first aid kit under the sink if you need it."

"Shut up, assholes!" Logan said, folding his arms. "Are we going to watch the movie or not?"

Caleb led Gabe to the tall, wooden cabinet next to the projector screen. He opened it to reveal shelves stacked with a variety of electronics, flashing black boxes with mysterious screens and hidden purposes.

"Oh, that's killer!" Gabe grinned, holding his laptop with one arm. "Your dad has a VHS player! We should find an old copy of *Halloween* or something and watch it this fall."

"What's a VHS player?" James asked from his seat.

Caleb was on his knees untangling an HDMI cable. "It's like a cassette player," he said, tapping a dark grey box about halfway up the stack, "except with movies instead of music."

"Oh, okay," James said, then turned to Logan. "What's a cassette player?"

Evan's eyebrows raised and concern once again morphed his face. Gabe plugged the HDMI into his laptop and sat it down beside the cabinet. He double-tapped the trackpad, and the screen went dark with a progress bar at the bottom. Caleb pressed a button on a black box in the cabinet and the projector began casting the mirrored image of Gabe's laptop onto the colossal screen. Gabe plugged in his phone to charge through his laptop and then ran to take a seat in the back row by Evan. Caleb flicked off the lights and joined on the other side of Evan. In front of them, James and Logan sat a seat apart in the front row. The light from Logan's phone clicked off as the movie began.

An old-timey film reel countdown from five. Fiery violins screeched as the screen faded into a grainy black-and-white scene of an auditorium. Scientists in white lab coats stood on stage talking amongst themselves next to cabinets of electronics that rivaled the ones in Caleb's dad's cabinets were stacked here and there on stage. One with wild white hair and a thick mustache stood next to a table with a large white sheet covering a bulking shape.

In the audience, two rows of decorated military men smoking cigarettes and staring at the stage with concentrated gazes. Behind them were half a dozen rows of men in dark suits.

"What the hell!" James said, raising his arms. "Is the whole movie going to be this blurry black-and-white shit?"

"Looks like a documentary or some early found footage film," Gabe said, rubbing his chin. "Maybe it's just a flashback scene."

"I think it's cool," admitted Caleb. "This might be the oldest movie I've ever watched down here on the projector."

"Shut up!" Logan said over his shoulder. "They're saying something."

Evan sat silently with his arms folded. His hands gently rubbed his arms as he stared at the screen with unblinking eyes. His stomach twisted into a knot, but he couldn't look away.

A scientist with white hair and a mustache introduced himself as Dr. Hooke and wrote his name on a chalkboard. His voice grew louder as the violins faded. He pointed to the others and gave them commands. The grainy black-and-white image made it difficult to see the details of the room, but they looked to be in a large brick auditorium.

"What's he saying?" James asked.

Logan said, "Something about a laser, I think. And particles. Parallel universe?"

"Are they going to open up another dimension?"

"Maybe if you two shut the fuck up," Caleb said, "we'll find out!"

The doctor moved over to a bulking shape covered by a cloth on a table. Dr. Hooke shouted, "Behold!" as he pulled the cloth off with two sweeping hands. Beneath was a laser. It looked like an alien ray cannon with an array of lightbulbs, enormous gauges, tubes of fluids, and a muzzle that looked like a satellite dish.

"Gentlemen!" said Dr. Hooke. "*This* is the gateway to the future! By emitting light with this powerful laser, matched with a concentrated sound frequency, we have created the machine we call 'Ardenti Sonus' which means…the burning sound!"

He turned and wrote "The Burning Sound" on the board behind him. Below it, he drew a diagram representing the laser with a beam shooting from it. He added waves to represent sound passing through the beam.

"With this, we can open doors near or far. As far as the other side of the universal curtain. With precise calculations and programming, we can—"

"No! Stop!" A voice came from out of the frame. "That laser must be destroyed!"

The camera panned from the stage and past the audience to reveal a suited man jogging down the aisle. His face was severely scarred, and his left arm was held in a sling. The camera followed him up to the stage where he confronted the doctor.

"You need to get these people out of here and destroy the laser before it's too late!" He yelled. Dr. Hooke stared daggers back down at him.

"Who the hell is this?" a gravelly voice yelled from the crowd.

"Gentlemen," Dr. Hooke said. He cleared his throat, composed himself, and pointed to the heckler. "This is one of my old colleagues, Dr. Browning.

He was fired for…gross negligence during an experiment, and so he holds a grudge. Pay him no mind as security escorts him out."

The doctor then motioned to the corners of the room for the man to be removed.

"Does this movie only have one camera?" James groaned. "Or did they not invent editing cuts by the fifties?"

"I like that it's one continuous shot," Gabe said. "It's harder to do, you know."

"Guys," Caleb said. "Shut it! They're talking."

"You must all leave!" Dr. Browning's face tightened as he pleaded to the audience. "Dr. Hooke is a madman! He doesn't know what he's playing with! This machine…it…it opened a portal to another dimension, and something came through from the world beyond where terror reigns! It attacked us and…and…took us into an uncanny, nightmarish reflection of our world, drained of light and life!"

A murmur drifted through the crowd. Dr. Hooke yelled from the stage, "Security! Remove this intruder!"

"THE BEING!" Dr. Browning screamed as two security guards grabbed him. "It snatched our team, one by one, and took them to Terror Zone! The demon paralyzed us with its glowing skull! My friends, they were all in comas when they began to — umph — get your hands off me!"

Browning fought the guards while being pulled down the aisle. The audience members turned their heads to watch. The camera followed, but Dr. Hooke could be heard off-camera saying,

"It's amazing the lengths some people will go through to sabotage a previous employer."

Quiet chuckles of agreement flowed through the crowd. One of the guards punched Browning's sling and he let out a wail. The other guard put a hand over Browning's mouth as they disappeared through the double exit doors. The camera panned back to the stage where Dr. Hooke stood with folded hands and a satisfied smile.

"Now, as I was saying, with precise calculations and programming, we can open a portal to the moon, to Mars, to Neptune, to wherever we wish in the far reaches of the universe! Nothing is too far! No destination too obscure!"

"What about what that other fellow said?" a voice from the crowd asked offscreen. "Is it dangerous?"

"Well," one of the doctor's colleagues said in a wavery voice as he stepped toward the front of the stage. "There was one instance—"

"Absolutely not!" Dr. Hooke looked back at his colleague, who lowered his head and took a step back. The doctor adjusted his lab coat and retained his showman demeanor and smile. "We've heard noises from certain frequencies, but nothing more than the equivalent of a thunderstorm."

"Let me get this straight," came a voice from the audience. "You're going to travel to *Mars* with that?"

Dr. Hooke's smile faded. He sighed and straightened his coat collar.

"Well, no," he admitted. "At least not with one this size. We would need a larger regulator One suited for a greater power consumption and — "

"What would be the point of traveling so far?" asked an authoritative voice. "There's nothing out there but rocks and frozen wasteland. There'll be no military or technological advantage for such a trip."

"On the contrary, General," said the doctor, loosening his tie as his face darkened. There is much more to gain than technological or military advancements. Think of the scientific discoveries. Imagine the new insights about the universe we could grasp. Answers to the most complex questions in science!"

"Oh, I see the benefit," the voice replied. The camera panned to include the front row, where a heavyset general with a heavily decorated uniform spoke up. "If we can perfect it, as you claim, we could teleport troops across enemy lines without their knowing. We could take out heinous world leaders and snuff out armies without stepping foot in a war zone. It's brilliant!"

"No, no, no," Dr. Hooke pleaded, now putting a hand to his forehead. "That's not at all the intent — "

"If we get it right, we could house a base on the moon," said a suited man with a high voice sitting in the third row. "That would give us immense gains on the battlefield. From that vantage point, we could fire a rocket and hit any spot in the world!"

"What the hell are they talking about?" Logan leaned over to James.

Evan looked away from the screen and saw James shake his head.

"Something about space travel," he said. "It all sounds crazy, even for a fifties sci-fi."

"The acting is pretty good," Gabe chimed in. "That Dr. Browning guy was a bit over-the-top though. It's classic bad acting, but the guy playing Hooke is killing it!"

"Shut up, guys!" Caleb said, leaning forward to rest his elbows on his knees. "I don't need the commentary."

Evan's eyes returned to the screen. His cheeks were hot and there was a pit in his stomach. He wished they'd keep talking about the movie, what they liked and didn't like, because it made it feel more like an actual movie. Otherwise, he wasn't too sure it was just a movie. It felt far too real for his tastes.

"Gentlemen, you must listen!" Dr. Hooke said on the screen, but his voice was overwhelmed by the clamor in the audience. The doctor's face darkened, and his eyebrows turned down in anger. The camera zoomed in on the stage, fixating on the scientist's rage.

"Now, Dr. Hooke," said the voice of the general as the voices simmered, "I think we've shown our interest in your laser, but if you want to secure funding for such a weapon, we must see a demonstration. Something worth our while. I mean, by God, all this excitement and potential goes down to hell if you don't have something semi-functional already."

Dr. Hooke stood before the group with his head hanging and arms folded. He was distraught, but at the request of a demonstration he raised his head and a silent grin spread across his face. The madman's widening eyes stared into the audience. His expression, the look in his eyes...something was building in his mind. Something sinister. Something evil. Something like a crazed second wind rising from the deep.

"You would like to see a demonstration?" Dr. Hooke said with a growing smile. "A demonstration...to put your mind at ease?"

He turned to his colleagues and waved to them. They exchanged a look then hesitantly set to work connecting power cables and turning dials on devices in the electronic cabinets. The doctor turned a large knob on the laser. The machine began to whirr, and the lights brightened.

"This is all pretty low budget," Logan said over his shoulder. "There's no soundtrack or anything."

"Then let's turn it off!" Evan blurted out, making the rest of the boys jump. "I mean, this is really lame, right?"

Logan narrowed his eyes at Evan and grinned. "Are you scared?" He laughed and turned back to the screen. "It's kind of lame, but it looks cool. I like it so far, score or no score."

"Me, too," Gabe said elbowing Evan. "You picked a good one, Ev."

"Yeah! Nice one, slugger!" James yelled over his shoulder without turning around.

The sound of the science equipment powering on ramped up, and the theater's surround sound speakers made it feel like Evan was in the auditorium with Dr. Hooke.

"It's like old-school sci-fi," Caleb said, looking down at his phone and rubbing his chin. "But I can't find it on IMDB. Must be an older cult movie or something. Maybe we could do a review video and post it online!"

Evan shifted in his seat and swallowed the worried fear that stuck in his throat like a knife.

"I think we should turn it off," he said.

"Holy shit, Evan!" James said, turning around. "You're scared? Of this?"

"You're kidding, right?" Logan laughed. "It's just a bunch of dudes talking about a laser."

"Guys!" Evan said, leaning forward. Unconsciously, he found himself shouting. "I think there's something wrong with the movie!"

"Come on, man," Caleb said as he leaned over toward Evan. "Chill out. It's just a movie. I want to see what happens."

"Yeah, let's shut up," Gabe said, shooting a look at Evan. He adjusted his long black hair and replaced the Raiders hat back on his head. "That doctor dude is about to start the laser!"

The boys turned their attentions back to the screen and Evan shriveled down in his seat. He stared up at the scientists as tall as elephants as they moved across the giant screen preparing the demonstration. The unsettling Dr. Hooke stood in the middle of the stage and turned toward the crowd. From the camera angle, it looked as though he were addressing the boys themselves.

"Gentlemen!" the mad doctor said. His gaze turned directly to the boys through the camera. "Brace yourselves, but do not panic. We are about to begin!"

Evan gripped his armrest. His eyes burned from staring, but he couldn't blink or turn away. The pit in his stomach ached. Something bad was going to happen. Very bad. He braced himself for what was coming.

"Now," the doctor continued, "as explained before, Ardenti Sonus is powered by an exorbitant amount of electric power to generate both the laser and the sound waves. Both require protection. Under your seats, you will find eye and ear protection, and I suggest you put them on now...or suffer your senses!"

After equipping his own eye and ear protection, he turned to the laser and flipped a series of switches. The laser responded with a low hum and a display of flashing lights from the laser's muzzle. The lights blinked several times before becoming one steady glow.

"The excessive power flowing to the laser creates a burning light," Dr. Hooke explained, his voice raising as the machines grew louder. "These large speakers behind me can emit frequencies near twenty hertz, mimicking that of an earthquake. When we couple it with the laser, we can expand or focus the light and manipulate new frequencies.

"These frequencies are the key to opening portals! By enlarging the light, we can open doors to great distances, even as far as the edge of the universe. And if we focus the light..." he said, pausing as he flipped a large switch on the laser with both hands. It whirred to life like an alien spacecraft about to take off. "We can open curtains to neighboring universes, those just outside our view!"

The laser's light glowed to match the fury of the sun. Even in black and white, the laser's brightness was almost blinding on the large projector screen.

Next came chaos.

The camera panned away from the intense light to the crowd. Members of the audience who hadn't yet donned their shaded goggles quickly strapped them to their faces or simply held them up in front of their eyes. The poor souls who didn't raise them in time grabbed at their eyes and wailed in pain, turning their heads away.

Evan put his own hands over his ears as the static revved through the speakers. His eyes stung from the brightness of the screen. He squinted and looked away.

On screen, the members of the audience without earplugs were subjected to the unmerciful fate of the deep sonic frequencies. Unprotected eardrums ruptured around the room, sending screams throughout the crowd. Hands went to ears as blood burst out, dripping down jaw lines like helmet straps. One of the men vomited from the pain while others simply collapsed to the floor. The crowd left standing began pushing and shoving past each other, heading to the exit in a panic.

"Goddamn!" Gabe yelled over the sounds. "These special effects are killer!"

"Dude, check out the blood," Caleb yelled back, his own hands over his ears. "The practical effects are realistic for the fifties! The sound's lousy, though! It keeps going fuzzy when it gets too loud."

The men in the first row of the audience were as petrified and as fascinated as the boys. They sat watching the laser as the camera panned back to the stage. The laser whirred and pulsed like a scream. Scientists scurried around on the stage, unsure of what to do as electronic cabinets began sparking and needled gauges gyrated back and forth like windshield wipers.

Dr. Hooke stood near the laser, a crazed captain steering his vessel into the heart of the storm. The flashing lights reflected in his shaded goggles while his lab coat blew backward from the force. A smile stretched across his face, and a laugh grew in unison with the laser's sparks and static.

Finally, the camera managed to capture the trajectory of the laser. On the far brick wall splattered a blob of what looked like molten lava. Without color, it was hard to tell just what was happening. Was it melting the brick? Something liquid, bright and stretching, dripped from the spot in the wall where the laser was pointed. As the beam burned brighter, it also bled upward like a crack in the wall. Soon, there was a jagged fracture climbing the wall, growing wider as it inched toward the ceiling.

Then came the sound.

It was like the freight-train winds of a tornado. Gales with the force of a hurricane blew through the auditorium like an invisible hand. Scientists, audience members, scientific equipment, and the laser cannon blew backward in an effortless push with godlike intensity.

Suddenly, the camera shook as if it had been knocked off balance. Something off-screen had hit it, and the new angle showed more of the room, including bodies and blood flying through the air. Heads, arms, and legs cracked against furniture, the stage, and the metal beams that supported the room. The wind remained constant, sweeping chairs and papers into the far corners of the auditorium.

The screeching winds reached a monumental peak and then stopped suddenly.

Caleb and Gabe exchanged glances with uneasy grins. Evan looked at them both and blurted out, "We shouldn't be watching this! Something's not right!"

Logan turned over his shoulder. Evan thought he would yell at him for being a coward, but his eyes were shifty, and his mouth quivered. He looked the way Evan felt. Logan quickly turned back around when Caleb leaned over to talk to Evan.

"Dude, it's just a movie," he gulped. "A very scary movie, sure, but...you know, you can go sit in the bar if you want. I don't think anyone would —"

A hollow growl filled the theater.

All eyes turned back to the screen where the remaining living scientists pushed themselves up and staggered to their feet. They looked upon the gigantic glowing rip in the wall with panicked faces as the monster from the movie's poster emerged.

THE BEING.

It crawled out of the crack in the wall. It moved onto the stage, standing taller than any man, with six skeletal limbs and a grinning, glowing skull for a face. It walked like an ape on its hind legs, but two other pairs of arms stretched out in front of it as if it had gone through some demonic mutation.

The screaming skull and scorched earth from the poster flashed in Evan's mind along with the letters in all caps and the frightening font.

*BEWARE THE BEING!*

Pitch-black skin covered its bony limbs. The dark complexion nearly disappeared into the shadowy background. Bleeding skin receded like a hood around the bright white skull face, which blazed with the same intensity as the portal. The creature opened its mouth full of teeth in a gaping yawn and again bellowed a deep hollow roar. It stretched out its four upper limbs, displaying its skeletal arms and long clawed fingers on each hand.

"Oh, my god! Oh, my god," Evan dug his fingernails into the leather cushions. "Oh, my god! Oh, my god."

Without warning, the beast charged the survivors.

Evan gasped. At his side, Gabe crossed his arms and Caleb put a hand over his mouth. James sat quietly, shaking his head uncontrollably. Logan pulled out his phone to distract his attention from the screen but bit his nails in clear dismay.

Evan's breathing became shallow. He wanted to cry, but his unblinking eyes stung in their sockets.

The creature's long, sharp fingers jabbed into scientists like knives. Fountains of dark blood sprayed from their lacerations and innards splattered to the floor. Others stared too long at the glowing skull and dropped into a coma-like state. The skull caught one man from behind and bit off his screaming head with a crunch and grind. His body wobbled a few steps before collapsing to the floor and gushing blood from the severed neck. Others were dismembered by sharp chomps by the skull's teeth or pulled apart by its bony hands.

Those left alive—or mostly alive—were dragged and thrown into the portal. Their screams warped before cutting off completely as their bodies disappeared into the void. They left behind only a series of bloody drag marks leading to the portal through a field of broken bones and spilled guts.

Evan knew the images would haunt him for the rest of his life, but he couldn't look away. He stared up at the screen, watching as the projector displayed shadows in various shapes over the pulsing light.

One single thought circled in his mind: *This. Is. Real.*

A screaming audience member bumped the camera again, which now showed the destroyed auditorium while the demon continued to ravage the men offscreen.

It was somehow worse to only hear the ripping of limbs, the gnawing of flesh, and the splatter of blood without seeing its destruction.

With one final bump, the camera fixed its gaze on the crack in the wall. The portal pulsed with a slow hypnotic glow. Soon, the hollow screams and growls stopped along with the screams of the dying victims. A low hum from the crack in the wall—the world beyond the curtain—grew louder, accompanied by the sound of static.

The boys sat paralyzed in their chairs with their eyes glued to the screen.

"Holy shit!" Caleb screamed above the static. "Is it over?"

Gabe shouted. "There's no way it's over. Probably just getting started."

Evan shot a look at Gabe out of the corner of his eyes. He prayed to God it wasn't just getting started.

"It looked real," Gabe continued to shout. "It's crazy good effects for back then. Makes *Night of the Living Dead* look like *House on Haunted Hill*."

"I think it is real!" Evan yelled through a clenched jaw. The tears he held back finally swelled and began to fall. "We need to turn it off. Now!"

The last of his words were drowned out by the static. By now, it had grown into a deafening roar. On screen, the portal pulsed and glowed like fire. Now, it didn't look like part of the screen, but part of the basement wall itself!

Evan jumped to his feet and screamed.

"Something's wrong! You've got to shut it off right now!"

With the static so loud, there was no way they heard what he said, but Gabe nodded with fear-stricken eyes and covered his ears. He yelled something at Evan and Caleb, then ran out of the aisle to his laptop. The portal pulsed brighter.

Caleb put his fingers in his ears. James and Logan turned around in their seats with their eyes watery from the brightness of the screen. Evan slumped down in the aisle with his palms planted over his ears like a little boy protesting a command from his mother.

At the cabinet of electronics, Gabe gritted his teeth as the nearest speaker blared in his ears. He pulled out his laptop. Gabe tried turning the volume down. The volume bar dropped on the unit's display, but the sound levels persisted. Evan saw him stop and cover an ear with his hand, mouthing a series of curse words. He was obviously frustrated as he banged away at his keyboard.

In a last-ditch effort, he yanked the cable from the laptop. The sound died instantly like a bullet to the head.

Gabe turned to the screen as the boys lowered their hands from their ears. The image remained on the screen, and the portal continued pulsing its glowing evil.

"Jesus," Caleb said, standing with his hands out and mouth agape. "What the hell happened?"

"I don't know," Gabe said, panting. He sat his laptop down on a shelf and raised his hat to adjust his long hair. "I'm just glad the sound's gone. That static was—"

"Guys!" James said, turning back to the bright screen. "I still hear something."

Evan peeked over the seat in front of him and began to tremble. Sounds still seeped from the speakers. No, not the speakers...the screen! The sounds came directly from the images on the screen! Evan heard deep hollow growls and screams from off-screen as if a prowling lion lay just behind the projector sheet.

The growls were those of an unsatisfied monster. Objects in the unseen room could be heard being moved around in reckless abandon. Metal chairs clanged into each other. Broken glass shattered on the floor. A table screeched against the floor then broke with a loud boom. The creature was searching for something. Or someone. It groaned and then became distant. The room was again quiet.

"What the hell is going on?" Caleb said, staring at the screen with squinted eyes.

"This is a fucked-up movie," Logan said, turning back to the screen.

"I don't think it's a movie," Evan blubbered, wiping the tears from his eyes. "I think it's...I think it's...I think it's...."

"Real." Gabe finished for him in a distant voice. He replaced his hat on his head and stared at the screen. "Maybe we should unplug the projector."

"Okay," Caleb nodded and gulped. "Okay. I'll try that."

He passed Evan, who hunkered down in the aisle in a fetal position. James and Logan turned around to watch as Caleb put a foot on each center seat's armrest and reached for the projector. His back was turned to them, and his arms stretched up for the power cable.

Behind him on the screen, the crack in the wall pulsed with the same fiery, ominous glow. Then came the deep hollow growl from beyond, like approaching thunder in the distance. Now a storm of galloping footsteps accompanied it, matching the rhythm of Evan's heart trying to beat out of his chest.

"Holy shit!" James and Logan said, looking at each other.

Gabe's eyes followed the sound as it moved through the speakers.

"Fuck!" he said.

"Shit balls!" Evan blurted out.

"Jesus, Evan!" James yelled back to him.

The light from the screen changed. It darkened over their faces like rain clouds. Then came a sinister sunshine. They all turned to the screen.

THE BEING stood in front of the crack in the wall. Four arms swung slowly from its torso like dead tree branches swaying in an unsettling winter wind. The glowing skull pulsed just as the fissure had, framed by the bleeding skin around it. The boys stared at the horror on the screen, and though its sockets were empty, the creature stared right back.

"Pull the plug!" Gabe screamed.

Caleb broke his trance and went back to the projector, rising on tiptoe to reach the cables in back. The demon's face raised up in his direction, watching him as it raised its four black, skeletal arms.

"Hurry, goddammit!" Gabe yelled.

Just as Caleb's fingertips touched the power cable at the back of the hanging projector, THE BE-ING reached out its arms. The long black hands grabbed the bottom edge of the screen like a ledge, its claws reaching out beyond the screen and into the room. The creature pulled itself closer to the screen as if to leap out at them!

A monstrous hand shot out and seized Caleb's leg with fingers like ropes. He yelped and grabbed at the fingers to pry them off as they pulled him down.

James and Logan screamed and climbed up and out of their seats. Before they could flop into the second row, a single hand reached through the screen, grabbed them by the legs and pulled them down. The boys bawled in pain and fear, their legs caged in the grip of the beast's fist. They kicked and twisted.

Evan let out a bloodcurdling scream. He couldn't believe what he was seeing!

The grinning skull pushed through the screen and released a breathy roar. Behind it, the portal's light shined brightly, and the static filled the air again. The demon's other two hands shot out, searching for Gabe and Evan.

"Get out of the aisle!" Gabe screamed and pulled Evan from the floor.

The demon reached out further. The sound of static washed over them, and the projector's light burned hotter in the room. The skull moved toward them. Gabe tried pushing Evan away from the hands, but it was too late. The hands knocked them both to the ground and pinned them. Evan's glasses went askew, and air escaped his lungs. He heaved and gasped, but the weight was crushing, making it hard to breathe.

Suddenly, the hands began to drag them toward the screen. Evan screamed and pulled his hand free. He grabbed at the carpet, but the threads burned through his fingers as the demon pulled him away. Beside him, Gabe kicked and squirmed, trying to knock himself loose.

Caleb lunged at the overhead projector and tugged it while resisting the monster. The light rocked with each pull. The boys' screams were drowned out by the demon's hollow roar behind them.

The hand holding James and Logan pulled toward the screen. The two boys cried out as they were jerked into the auditorium with the monster and flung into the fiery sun of the portal.

THE BEING grinned, protruding from the wall as if leaning into the theater room through a window.

Evan noticed the projector light flicker, pulsing on and off in slow blinks. Then he was pulled backward and consumed in blinding light. Through the static, he heard Caleb screaming his name.

Then there was darkness.

# THREE

Gabe opened his eyes. Waking in a slow stupor, it took several deep breaths to get his body moving. He was lying on the floor in a painful collapse. With harsh blinks, he began to look around him.

He saw Evan behind him, lying like a contortionist. A soft snore let Gabe know he was still among the living. In the first row of the theater, a pair of Under Armour socks moved back and forth in a slow, waking manner. At least James was still alive, and Logan wouldn't be too far from him, but he'd have to get up to find Caleb. His scream was the last thing he remembered before. . .

Gabe shuddered and wobbled to his feet, giving Evan a shake on his way up.

Evan looked up at Gabe and then jumped back where he lay. His head darted from side to side, then he sat up and adjusted his glasses, which were crooked on his face. Gabe almost hated to wake him. He was peaceful while asleep, but now he seemed jittery like an anxious raccoon.

In the front row, James stood and stretched in the projector light and Logan muttered something about his hair. They were alright. Gabe's chest was tight, but he tried to keep his cool. He looked at the projector, stared at it, and felt his heart quicken. As James approached him, he attempted to slow his breathing and rubbed his eyes.

"What the hell happened?" Logan finally popped his head up over the seat. He was combing his hair with quick practiced movements.

It was then that Gabe noticed something different about Logan's blond hair. It was gray. Logan looked like an old man with a baby face and his green button-up was pale. For that matter, the red of James's hat had dulled into a dark gray, too. His Ozark Baseball shirt was drained of its red and white as well.

"Guys," Gabe said in a shaking voice. "Your clothes…"

They looked at each other, confused. They didn't understand.

"The color," Gabe said carefully. "It's…it's —"

" — gone," Evan said, sitting against the back wall, pulling his knees against his chest. The shakiness in his voice overshadowed Gabe's. "You guys look dead!"

They looked again, but this time, it registered for them. Their mouths dropped open. Logan jumped back, tripping into one of the seats.

"What the fuck is going on?" he yelled. He pulled at his shirt, staring down with panicked eyes. Locks of his hair fell again, and his fingers immediately went to fixing them. James looked down at his own shirt. His eyes looked up and down, then over at Gabe and Evan, before finally turning to the screen.

The portal's glow pulsed in silence. The image on the screen was sharper, clearer, more real. The fissure was now part of the screen, and the colors had changed. Rather, there *was* color. The pulsing light had become a bright orange and yellow glow, almost like flames.

"Holy shit," Logan whispered, fingers woven in his hair. "We're not in Missouri anymore."

"What *was* that thing?" James turned to Gabe and frowned. "I can still feel its fingers around me…"

He wrapped his arms around his torso and stared at the floor, a mournful look touching his face.

"It was THE BEING!" Evan spoke up, biting his lip. "That skeleton thing from the movie."

Gabe shook his head and looked up at the projector screen.

"THE BEING," Gabe repeated. "The poster tried to warn us in all caps."

*BEWARE THE BEING!*

"Did it kill us, man?" Logan blurted out. He pulled his feet into the seat and looked like a mental patient about to rock back and forth. "Are we fucking dead?"

"Shut up, Logan!" Gabe yelled.

Logan's mouth moved up and down, then closed with a quiver. He brought his chin down and continued running through his hair.

"Where's Caleb?" Evan asked, looking frantically around the basement as he emerged from his fetal position.

Gabe turned to the back row.

"Caleb?" he said, heading to the seats. His heart skipped a beat when he got no reply and then sped up when he realized Caleb wasn't there.

"Where the hell is he?" James asked.

"Probably got scared and shit his pants," Logan said, peeking up from his chair. "Same as the rest of us."

"Caleb!" Evan called into the basement. He got to his feet and went to the far wall to flip on the light. Nothing happened, even after four or five flicks. "Guys, the power's out."

"No, it's not, you idiot," James said, shaking his head. "The projector's still on!"

Gabe shook his head and started to say something when a bump came above them. They all stared at the ceiling as if something had appeared there. They listened. Another few bumps traveled across the floor and then disappeared. The boys looked at each other with gaping mouths and fearful eyes.

Gabe swallowed. "I think it pulled us into its world."

"*Its* world?" Logan questioned, tilting his head to one side. "Like, through the movie? It looks a hell of a lot like ours."

"Dr. Browning," James said. He was looking at the sports memorabilia on the wall. "That guy said they were pulled into a reflection of their world or something. Maybe that's what happened to us."

Gabe looked around.

"Shit!" Logan had his phone out, tapping its blank screen repeatedly. "My phone's not working. There's no way it could be dead already! I charged it in Mr. Thompson's class before we left school."

James pulled his phone from his pocket. "Mine's dead, too. What the hell?"

His red cap with the Cardinals logo on the back was now an ashy gray with a bird bearing more resemblance to a raven than the St. Louis redbird. Gabe opened his mouth to point it out but decided to say nothing.

"I'm going to find Caleb," Evan said, standing up. His eyes were puffy, and he wouldn't look the other boys in the eye. "It sounded like he was upstairs, so—"

"Are you insane?" Logan hopped up and confronted him. "That wasn't Caleb. Caleb's dead! That was that damn demon skeleton!"

"Alright, back off!" Gabe stuck a hand on Logan's chest and pushed. Logan was caught off balance, but James caught him before he fell.

"You want to try that again?" Logan screamed.

"Dude," James told his friend. "Shut the hell up."

"We don't know if it's Caleb or that monster up-stairs," Gabe said, crossing his arms. "We can't just stay here in the basement if Caleb's up there and needs our help, but we're not going to split up. I've seen too many horror movies to do that."

No one argued, but Logan stared at Gabe a few moments before lowering his eyes and folding his arms.

"We need to get to Caleb," Evan piped up. "Before something bad happens to him."

"Fine. Go if you're going," Logan said, moving back to his chair.

"Nope," James grabbed his shoulder. "Gabe's right. Splitting up would be stupid. We need to stick together."

"But I—"

"Come on, Logan," Evan said, moving toward the stairs.

James turned back to Logan. "You okay knowing Evan has bigger balls than you?"

Logan frowned. "You know what? Fine! I'll go. But if I get eaten by the skull spider, I'm going to be pissed!"

The boys headed up the stairs. Their steps were steady, their ears listening.

Behind them, the portal pulsed in its orange and yellow light. It cast enough light up at the top of the stairs to guide their steps. At the top of the stairs, James tried the light switch.

No luck.

They entered the quiet, dark hallway on the first floor. Their socked feet made no sound on the stone floor. No lights worked, but here, at least, the faint light from outside shone in through the front windows of the house.

"Okay," Gabe said as the boys moved to a quiet huddle like an offensive timeout. "Where did the bumps come from?"

Logan shook his head and replied in a tense voice, "How the hell should we know?"

James looked over his shoulder, biting his bottom lip. "It was the back of the theater, but I'm not sure where that'd be up here."

Gabe opened his mouth to guess but saw Evan with a furrowed brow and chose instead to listen.

"The basement stairs go down and to the right," Evan said, leaning into the huddle, "then to the left side of the house. The screen is at the front of the house, so the bumps came from there."

His finger pointed the way to the dining room. Gabe smirked and then led the way.

They entered one by one, each of them marveling at the monochromatic room's dark wood dining set and hanging chandelier. To the left was an abstract painting hanging on the wall. Across from where they entered were two large windows with curtains framing the dimly lit view outside. To their right was a swinging door connecting to the kitchen.

"This is so weird," James said in timid awe. He stopped and stared at the painting. "The colors on the paintings are gone."

"It's supposed to be green and blue and yellow," Evan said in a small voice.

"Yeah, exactly," James nodded. "What was it the doctor in the movie said?"

Logan's eyes went wide, and his voice broke into a higher pitch. "Dr. Hooke?" he squeaked out.

"No, the other one," Gabe said, his eyes wandering about the painting. "Dr. Browning. He said they were pulled into a world drained of color and life."

He swallowed after the last word. It was exactly where they were. He shivered. Lightning flashed through the windows and a groan of rolling thunder gently shook the house. Gabe clenched his fists and gulped. Clearing his throat, he pulled his attention from the painting.

"Come on," he said, "let's keep moving."

They headed to the kitchen door and Gabe pushed it open about a foot before he stopped in his tracks. Evan bumped into him and nearly knocked him over.

"Hey," he whispered, "what's the—"

Gabe elbowed him in the stomach and put a finger to his lips with lightning speed. His eyes were big and round. He leaned into the doorway and his heart stopped. There in the kitchen it stood.

THE BEING.

It moved with lumbering steps and stood hunched over so its head didn't bump against the high ceiling. Its back was turned to the door where the boys stood. With its sharp, long-fingered hands, it touched everything it passed, leaving scratches and gashes. Gabe held his breath as it moved down the cabinet, its skull's glow illuminating the kitchen.

Gabe gasped when he saw that the demon held something in one of its hands: Caleb.

He lay limp, confined by the creature's long, bony fingers. Caleb's feet dragged the ground, and his head bobbed limply like a doll. Gabe wanted to look closer, to see if his friend moved of his own accord, but he was scared to lean any further into the kitchen.

Beyond the demon, he could see a picture of Caleb and Rachel stuck to the refrigerator with a magnet. They were on vacation, a little younger, and standing in front of the Garden of the Gods entrance sign. A tinge of sadness stung Gabe's chest. The picture might as well have been from a thousand years ago. He pulled his head out of the kitchen.

"Back!" he said, pushing the others back into the dining room. "We need to get out of here *now*!"

The door between the rooms swiveled back and forth and the beast's head shot up toward them. Its body crawled toward the door. It pushed open the door, reached into the dining room, and peered through the doorway.

"Come on!" Gabe said as the boys moved toward the hallway. His socked feet slipped as he tried to catch traction on the floors. Behind him, Logan nearly fell over, but he grabbed one of the chairs and righted himself. He pulled the chair as he stumbled, and it screeched across the floor. He released his grip, and the chair tipped over and fell with a loud clatter. The creature screamed and lunged for the chair, attacking it with fury, giving the boys time to rush out of the dining room.

Gabe led them down the hall and into the living room at the front of the house. There, they found a mammoth-sized fireplace and two leather sofas as long as cars with a large marble coffee table between them. Evan slipped under the coffee table. Logan ducked behind a wing-backed chair in the corner next to a bookcase. Gabe and James each stepped behind of the large French doors at the entrance to the room.

Gabe held his breath. His heartbeat thumped in his ears, matching the sound of each step the creature took through the house. He heard its hollow breathing echo through the stillness.

Through the gap in the door jamb the creature's dark body nearly disappeared in the darkness, but its grinning skull approached with a ghostly presence. One of the creature's hands carried Caleb as the others crawled along the wall and ceiling like giant, skeletal spiders hunting for their prey.

Gabe watched the creature stop and look around the hall. It stared at the front door, then turned and stared into the room where the boys hid. The eerie glow moved over the room, threatening to reveal their hiding spots.

Then, in a slow pan, the light moved in the other direction, and the boys were thrust into darkness again. The monster moved across the hall, where Gabe could see a large desk and some bookcases in the demon's glow.

Gabe breathed a sigh of relief. He looked across the doorway at James and saw a large decorative metal doorstop. Another sat in front of Gabe's door. This gave him the idea for their escape! He could use the doorstop to distract the monster. All he had to do was pick up his doorstop, step out into the hall, and throw it!

*Wait*, he thought, *I can't throw worth a shit.*

Gabe thought back to little league baseball. He couldn't throw it straight, let alone anywhere worth trying. However, behind the opposite door stood a star baseball player with a killer swing and an award-winning throwing arm.

With the creature's attention turned elsewhere, Gabe decided now was their chance. He leaned out from behind the French door and waved a hand in James's direction. James peeked his head out.

*The doorstop!* Gabe mouthed to James, pointing down at the boy's feet.

James looked down, saw the stop, then nodded.

*Pick it up,* Gabe mouthed in exaggerated mouth movements, *and throw it!*

James first nodded slowly, then shook his head vigorously as the crazy plan formed in his mind. He flipped Gabe the bird and mouthed, *fuck you.*

Gabe threw his hand up in a frustrated shrug.

Their silent argument lasted only seconds before James complied. He bent down and pulled the doorstop from beneath the door and leaned into the hall. He then raised his arm and chucked it up the stairs. He booked it back behind the door as the stop bumped three times somewhere above.

THE BEING emerged from the office and charged up the stairway, bellowing its hollow roar and fumbling its arms about. Its claws scraped the steps and wall as it went, sending chunks of sheet-rock tumbling down the stairway.

Gabe heard crashing upstairs followed by a shrill screech of static feedback. After more banging, the screech stopped, and the demon roared. It ransacked the upstairs and the boys remained in their hiding places for several minutes until the sound moved far enough away.

They were safe, for now.

"Holy shit!" James said as they emerged from their hiding places. "I thought I'd botch that for sure!"

"What the hell was that thing?" Logan said, shaking.

"Did you see Caleb?" Gabe said between heavy breaths.

"I think he's dead," Evan admitted.

"No!" Logan shouted, then hushed himself and rubbed his neck.

"I'm not so sure," Gabe said. "It's hard to tell."

"Whatever," Evan said. His eyes became glossy, and the coloring of his face darkened. "I think it's time we got out of here and went to the police."

"Evan!" Logan said in a harsh, hushed voice. "You're being too loud. Shut the fuck up!"

"No," Evan said, wiping his eyes and moving to the door. "I'm getting on my bike and getting the shit out of here."

"Evan, wait!" Gabe said, but he was already through the doorway. Gabe followed him, ever conscious of the stairway as he passed.

Evan stopped just outside. The other boys followed him out onto the front porch steps and wished they hadn't. They stood outside the house with a front-row seat to the apocalypse.

The neighborhood was gone. Instead, the house sat in a desert of ashes and glistening coals. In each direction Gabe turned, he saw only an endless sea of charred landscape and stormy gray skies. The clouds hung overhead, and a slow pulsing light glowed beyond them like that of the portal in the basement. Flurries of ash fell from the sky in big, fluffy flakes. In the far distance, darkness loomed. The isolation set in as the hope faded.

"Oh, my god," Gabe said. A chill of fear gripped his spine, a feeling that only worsened the longer he stared. "We're in Terror Zone."

"No, we're not," Logan said in a quavering voice. "We're in hell!"

The boys stood with gaping mouths gazing at the burned wasteland before them. Their eyes widened and their lips quivered. No one spoke as ash fell like snow on their heads.

# FOUR

"My phone still works!" Gabe said as he held his phone to the other boys. It was still plugged into his laptop. "I only have one bar, but I've got to try calling her."

He was standing in front of the electronics cabinet in the basement, pacing back and forth as he spoke. Logan and James were sitting in the theater's back row. They had just finished barricading the door with all the chairs from the bar and were still catching their breaths. James rubbed his neck and Logan was running his fingers through his hair, but Gabe suspected it was more of an attempt to calm down than to fix his appearance. Evan sat against the wall with his knees to his chest and his arms folded on top.

"I don't understand." James held up his own phone. "Ours have been dead since we got here and there's no way there's a Verizon tower in Terror Zone."

Gabe shook his head. "I'm not sure. Maybe because it was plugged into the laptop it's still connected to our world somehow."

"I get it," Logan said. "We need to call somebody, but why Rachel? Why not the police? Or Caleb's parents?"

"Or our parents," Evan said. The others said nothing. Gabe figured ignoring him somehow felt almost worse than teasing him, but he didn't have time to feel sorry for hurting his feelings. Evan regressed further into his own arms.

"I don't even know my parents' numbers," James admitted. He saw the look from the other boys and said, "What? It's on my phone. I never thought to memorize it."

"I don't know how long my phone will stay on, and I want someone who can come help if they answer. Caleb's parents are out of town, so they're out," Gabe said. "My parents are an hour away. My brother is away at college, or he'd be the perfect person to call."

"And that leaves Rachel?" James said.

Gabe nodded. "That leaves Rachel," he sighed. "Look, she was supposed to be here tonight."

"What do you mean?" James turned in his chair. "Like, was she supposed to babysit us or something?"

Gabe shrugged and folded his arms. "Something like that, but she didn't. She wanted to go to her friend's house and Caleb wanted us to have the house to ourselves. So, she'll be in deep shit if her parents find out she left us alone."

"We're fourteen," James stood up and raised his voice at Gabe as if he made the rules. "We don't need a babysitter!"

"Calm the hell down," Gabe stepped up to him, almost putting his forehead against the bill of James's cap. "We've got bigger problems than crappy parents."

He thought James might push him or yell in his face, but the anger in his demeanor diminished, and James stepped back to his chair. It wasn't much of a battle, but Gabe felt his chest puffed out anyway. He felt confident and strong, though James's athletic build suggested he'd win in a real fight.

"So what if she gets in trouble," Evan said, peeking from his turtle shell. "We lost Caleb. We're trapped here. Isn't this an emergency?"

Gabe took out his phone and the screen illuminated his face. The signal was low, but as he stepped closer to the projector screen it became stronger.

"I want to give her a chance," he said, not looking up. "She took a risk to give us a private party, even if she didn't want to be here in the first place."

"Well, how do we call her?" James asked. "Do you even have her number?"

"I've got it," Gabe said, waving his phone to the group.

"Really?" Logan said. "Mind giving it to me when you get done?"

"She doesn't like baby carrots," Gabe said without missing a beat.

"Only you'd think of girls at a time like this." James shoved Logan off the seat next to him. "They don't even like you."

Logan opened his mouth then shut it and looked away.

Gabe pressed his phone screen and put it to his ear. The dial tone was quiet and cut in and out. He stepped into the light of the projector. Suddenly, the tone was steady in his ear.

"It's ringing!" He nearly laughed at how excited he was, and he briefly wondered when the last time he even used his phone to call someone.

Gabe chewed his lip and closed his eyes to listen. The other boys watched him in quiet anticipation. The ring was a muffled hum in a sea of silence. After a minute, Gabe started to lower the phone to hang up when a voice came over the phone.

"Hello?"

Her voice was dull and distant, but familiar. Gabe's chest relaxed at its sound and his grin returned.

"Rachel?" He pulled the phone from his ear to put it on the speakerphone.

"Gabe?" the voice whispered.

"Rachel! Can you hear me?"

Gabe pressed rapidly at his volume keys. Her voice was so quiet he could hardly hear it.

"Rachel!" he said with his mouth to the mic. "Are you there?"

It was quiet for a moment—so quiet he thought he'd lost her—then her voice came low and soft. It sounded like she was in a trance.

"Gabe?" she said. "Aren't you at Caleb's sleepover?"

"Yes!"

"You totally woke me up. I was dead asleep."

Another voice crackled over the phone, a sleepy male voice that startled Gabe and made his ears hot with embarrassment. Gabe heard the voice mumble, "Babe? Babe, what are you—"

"Nothing," Rachel said. "It's Gabe."

"Gabe?" the voice said, some alarm in his sleepy words. "Who the hell is—"

"He's like twelve," Rachel said. "Don't worry about him."

*I'm fifteen,* Gabe thought, shaking his head. James rolled his eyes and sank down into his chair. Logan leaned in further to hear better.

"Sounds like her *friend* turned out to be a boyfriend," Logan said, elbowing James.

"I can hardly hear her," said Evan, who sat up out of his fetal position. His round eyes and hopeless face hadn't improved.

"Rachel!" Gabe tried to get her attention. "We need your help!"

There was a pause on the phone, long enough that Gabe woke the screen in fear the call had dropped. It was still connected, timer counting, and Rachel began to groan like a grumpy toddler.

"Mmm," she said. "I ordered you guys pizza, right?"

"Yeah, but something's happened."

"Did the projector stop working? Wi-Fi out?" She was awake now and an annoyed attitude surfaced in her voice.

"No, but—"

"Is the house on fire?"

"No, Rachel." Gabe was getting frustrated.

"What, did somebody get hurt?"

Gabe stopped, unsure how to answer. "Yes" was probably the best answer, but he couldn't bring himself to simply say so.

"It's complicated," he said. "I mean, yes, but there's more to it than that."

"Where's Caleb?" she asked finally. "I want to chew his ass out for letting you call me."

Gabe opened his mouth but said nothing. He looked at the others with heavy eyes.

"We lost Caleb," he said.

"Lost him?" Rachel said. "What the hell are you talking about?"

"We watched a movie, and this thing came out and..." Gabe swallowed. "And it took him."

"Watched a movie?" Rachel was fully awake now, exasperated from the sound of it and getting increasingly more so as the call continued. "You're...not making...damn sense and I can barely he...you. What...ell's going o—"

Gabe's lip began to tremble as he looked helplessly at the other boys. Their faces became shadowy as the projector flickered and then darkened. Something was happening to their connection, and the light from the projector was dimming.

Quickly, Gabe tried to get out all he could as tears grew in his eyes. "Something came through the projector, and it grabbed Caleb and took off into the house," he said without taking a breath. "We don't have much time. We don't even know if he's still alive, but we have to—"

"—ear a damn thing...projector...breaking up..." Rachel's quiet voice was chopping up and sounded even more distant. "Coming home...not be some...beat your a—"

The call ended, and the projector screen flickered out. The boys screamed as they were engulfed in darkness.

"Goddammit!" Gabe threw his phone into the darkness and dropped to his hands and knees. He hadn't noticed, but he had started crying. The cold tears ran down his cheeks, and he felt them drop onto his clenched fists. He sobbed quietly and thanked God the lights were out so the others wouldn't see him. After a moment, he finally looked around the dark room. After wiping his eyes, the fear of loneliness crept in on him. A light came on and lit Evan's face like an angel in the dark.

"At least we tried," he said. His voice was small and shaky.

He had found Gabe's phone and now handed it back to Gabe. Gabe took it and turned on the flashlight, their one light in the dark basement.

He looked at the others. Logan sat clenching his knees to his chest, still fixing his hair compulsively. James leaned forward in the chair next to him, his hat drawn down and his arms folded. Evan was the only one looking Gabe in the eyes—eyes that were also glossy with tears. He wiped away tears of his own and got to his feet.

"You didn't scream."

Evan shook his head. "I did shut my eyes, though."

Gabe chuckled and turned to the projector screen. The large white canvas was blank, and the portal was gone.

"The portal on the screen," he said. "It must've been our way out. If only we weren't so chickenshit to try it."

James and Logan looked up to meet his gaze. Their distraught faces looked aged in the shadows of the flashlight.

"I think we need to find a way to get the projector back on," Gabe said.

"We can't leave Caleb," Logan said, choking on his friend's name. "He wouldn't leave us to be dragged around and eaten by some monster, dead or alive."

"I don't want to think about it" James replied with a quivering lip.

"Logan's right," Gabe said. "We can't leave Caleb if there's a chance that he's still alive."

They were quiet now, letting the seriousness of the situation sink in. Above them, distant thumps could be heard like groaning thunder. Gabe imagined the beast tromping around, looking for them.

He swallowed hard and shivered. It would probably devour Caleb soon, if it hadn't already.

The silence was as thick as the darkness around them, and then Logan spoke.

"We don't know if he's dead or alive," Logan said. "And either way, that monster will probably rip us to bits like those suckers in the..."

He stopped when he saw Gabe's face. It was reddening, but no tears were falling.

"Sorry," Gabe said. "I realize he could be dead — probably is — but if there's a chance he's still alive, we have to help him."

Gabe cleared his throat, fighting back tears to no avail.

"Caleb was with me a few years back," he said, "on the night I found my brother almost dead."

He saw other boys exchange glances, but they said nothing.

Gabe continued, dropping his eyes to the floor. "He was lying on the floor. We went down to his room in the basement for a movie. He used to let us sneak a movie for our sleepovers after my parents went to bed."

Gabe looked at the others and then looked back down at the floor.

"Anyway, we snuck down to his room and that's where we found him. There was a bottle of pills spilled into the carpet beside him. We thought he was dead. I was frozen. Couldn't move. Just dropped to my knees and started...bawling. I was worthless, but Caleb ran upstairs and woke my parents. Thank God he was there, otherwise my brother might not have..."

Gabe swallowed and coughed.

"I couldn't move," he pushed forward. "I love my brother, and I thought I'd lost him. I wanted to reach into his stomach and take the pills, to...I don't know.

"When the ambulance came, my parents went to the hospital with my brother. Caleb's parents came and picked him up, and he asked them to let me stay overnight. I ended up staying with them for months."

He looked up at James and Logan and cleared his throat.

"That's why I got held back a year. I missed a lot of school. That was two years ago, back when he lived by the ballpark in Ozark."

"I remember that place," Evan said. "It was over by Kissee Trails."

"There was a cute girl who lived by Kissee," Logan said.

"Mackenzie Warner! I forgot about her. I think she left for college. She had strawberry blond hair."

"And a nice curvy figure," Logan nodded with a smile.

"She played first base," James smirked and dazed dreamily at the ceiling. "But I would have loved to make it to second."

Logan leaned over to him and said, "I wouldn't have minded to Kissee *her* trails!"

The boys laughed, especially Gabe who let out a burst of amusement.

"Caleb was always there for me," Logan said with a sigh after they'd quieted down. "You know, he's the one who told me girls like sexy hair."

He ran his fingers through his high-volume hair and struck a pose. It got a chuckle out of the other boys despite the cheesiness.

"He invited me to my first major league game," James said, straightening his cap. "I went with him and his family to watch the Cardinals play the Royals in KC."

Gabe smiled. "Caleb told me about that," he told James. "He said you guys caught a foul ball in the ninth inning."

"Hell yeah!" James laughed. "Merrifield hit it right to us. The Royals won five to four. It was a good game. Still have the ball on a shelf in my room."

Logan looked away and James removed his hat and stared at the floor, hanging his head.

"I hate that this feels like a funeral," he said finally.

"It doesn't have to be." Evan hopped to his feet and stared down at them, pushing his glasses from the end of his nose. "Caleb was my first friend. I'd played with friends in elementary school, but it wasn't until he started copying off me in American History that anyone was nice to me on purpose."

He looked around and Gabe met his eyes. His own were wide and still glossy from tears. James and Logan said nothing and looked away.

"He was always the cool rich kid, what with his jokes and fancy stuff. Gave the best high fives, too, and tried to include me even if I wasn't wanted.

It felt good to be invited tonight." He smiled and shrugged. "Well, before all this crap, I mean."

Gabe stood and put a hand on Evan's shoulder.

"Well, Evan," he said. "You're a real friend to us. You're quirky jerky, as my brother would say, but we're glad you're here. I think it's safe to say once you experience a black-and-white horror adventure together, you're bound for life."

Gabe looked around. He had nearly forgotten until he said something. Just like watching black-and-white movies, it was surprising how quickly he had gotten used to a color-drained world.

"Let's go save our friend." James stood up and replaced his baseball cap. He gave Evan's shoulder a hearty punch. "What do you say, shit dick?"

The boys laughed. Evan grinned so wide that Gabe let loose a belly laugh and bent his head back. Logan giggled, leaned back on his hands, and let his hair fall on his brow.

"We're kind of fucked here anyway," Logan said, smiling and shaking his head. "We might as well die monster hunting. Chicks love a badass."

"Don't forget about saving Caleb," Evan insisted.

"Hell yeah," Logan said, standing with a confident smirk. "Let's save Caleb's ass!"

# FIVE

"It sounds easy," Gabe said, staring up the stairs at their makeshift barricade. "Slay the dragon and save the princess, but it'll be a wet-your-pants shit show. I'm sure of it."

"Do we have to split up?" Evan asked, adjusting his glasses. "I mean, you said it was a bad idea before."

"We don't know where it went. It's better to split up and cover more ground. Easier to hide with fewer people, too."

"But what if we find that skeleton demon thing and it attacks?"

"Scream really loud. We'll come distract him and lure him away. But you've gotta do the same for us." Gabe shook a finger at him like a child. "It's only fair."

Evan gulped and wiped sweat from his forehead.

"Well, if we're going to face that thing," James said, stepping to the wall of memorabilia, "I'm going down swinging."

He reached up and removed a wooden bat with the St. Louis Cardinals logo burned into the barrel. He took his time admiring it, hitting it against his palm to test the weight, then raised it to his shoulder with a smile. With his cap, he looked like he could have been a young rookie on the team. Gabe remembered something he'd said earlier in the night and chuckled.

"You'll finally get to know what it's like to bat in the major leagues," he told James.

James smirked and choked up on the bat. "Hell yes!"

Logan frowned and crossed his arms. "How do we know a bat is going to do any good? Can you even swing it hard enough?"

James scoffed, stepped to the cutout of Rocky, and swung the bat with a practiced stance. The wooden bat connected with the cardboard and folded the boxer, ripping him in half. James turned back with the bat on his shoulder, a pose reminiscent of the *Conan the Destroyer* movie poster behind him.

"Impressive." Logan began to slow-clap. "Except that fucker upstairs isn't made of cardboard."

"It's the best shot we have," Gabe said. "I say we each take something."

Evan stepped to the wall and grabbed another wooden bat. He held it away from him like a gun that could go off at any moment.

"It's not going to bite you," James laughed.

Evan frowned. "I know that. I just don't know if it's enough. I want a helmet, too."

"Take one," Gabe shrugged. "Caleb's dad's not here to hound you about touching his stuff."

With a smirk, Evan reached up and pulled a Chiefs helmet off the shelf. It was large on his head, but he looked battle-ready. He raised the bat and swung it. It hit the wall and he released his grip with a yelp. The wall was left with a fist-sized dent and the bat clanged to the ground and rolled away.

"Maybe I'll just take a couple balls," Evan said, heading back to the shelf. He reached up on tiptoes and grabbed an NFL football with a dozen or so signatures.

"Never too late to grow a pair," Logan said, picking up the bat. He swung it a couple of times. His swing wasn't as hard or practiced as James's, but it wasn't clumsy.

"We could all use an extra ball," Gabe said, grabbing another football. "Ours might be in our throats."

He looked around at the other boys, gladiators ready to face the coliseum. James stood admiring his bat, warming up his swing with a smirk that wouldn't go away. Logan held his bat on his shoulder and tossed a baseball up and down in his other hand. Evan had a football tucked under his arm and reached under his oversized helmet to adjust his glasses.

*What a team*, Gabe thought. They stood with their weapons in hand and faces underlined by fear but emboldened by bravery, ready to climb the stairs and hunt the beast.

"Let's go," Gabe said and headed up the stairs. The boys followed and helped move the barricade of chairs down to the landing, making sure they were accessible just in case they had to board up the door in a hurry.

Gabe stuck his head out of the basement door. The hallway was quiet, dark, dismal, and dead. There was no sign of the monster. He looked both ways like a kindergartener deciding if it was safe to run across the street. With no sign of life and no sounds about the house, he motioned for the others to follow him out into the battleground.

He turned to the boys once they entered the hall behind him. "Logan, you and Evan search down here. James and I will search upstairs—"

"I want James to come with me," Evan blurted out. He shut his mouth quickly, then lowered his gaze. His face turned the gray color of the Chief's helmet. "He's better with the bat."

"Well, thanks a lot, dingus," Logan said, giving him a push.

Gabe saw the look of fear on Evan's face, eyes shifty and beads of sweat glinting in the noir darkness. He leaned forward and put a hand on Logan's shoulder.

"It's okay. Logan and I can go upstairs," he said then turned to Logan. "You can search Rachel's room if you want."

Logan's eyebrows raised and his ears perked up.

"Well, what are we waiting for?" he asked with a smile. "Let's split up gang!"

Gabe and Logan began their ascent upstairs. Looking over the railing, Gabe watched as the star baseball player with the bat on his shoulder and the nerd with his oversized football helmet disappeared into the dining room. He said a quick half-prayer for them as he continued onward.

The stairway carpet softened their steps, but nothing could soften his fears as they climbed into the menacing dark of the upstairs hallway. They avoided stepping on the scratches left by the creature's claws and the chunks of sheetrock littering the steps. Gabe kept his guard up as his eyes searched the darkness. The hairs on his neck stood at attention. He felt like a SWAT officer entering a den of thugs. Danger could jump out at any moment.

They stepped onto the second floor. Instantly, they missed the carpeted stairs as cold hardwood greeted their socked feet. In front of them was a large four-pane window with a window seat decorated with pastel green blankets, stacked antique Charles Dickens and Jane Austen books, and fake daisies sticking out of a watering can—stylings courtesy of Caleb's mom. With the color now drained, it looked more like a gothic shrine than springtime decorations.

Outside the window, ash fell like snow against a distant fiery glow.

"I'll check Caleb's room," Gabe said softly as he moved to a busted door to the right. "You check Rachel's room down the hall, first door on the left."

Logan looked in the direction of Rachel's room. The same fiery light from outside flickered from the doorway into the dark hall like an eye searching for life. Gabe saw that Logan's eagerness to peruse a girl's room in her absence was gone, replaced with a dull gaze and a quivering lip.

"Maybe we shouldn't split up entirely," Logan said, his voice cracking on the last syllable. He swallowed hard, working his young Adam's apple. "You know, just in case we run into that thing."

Gabe opened his mouth to protest, but Logan's unease made him sigh with mercy.

"Alright. Just stay in the doorway and keep watch."

Logan accepted the task and Gabe entered Caleb's room. The door was busted off its hinges, and the room had been dismantled. It looked like a clip from a crime movie where the police show up to the scene of a murder and the house looks as if a tornado had just passed through. In this case, it had.

Just inside the bedroom lay the doorstop. Gabe picked it up and examined the area. The creature had climbed the stairs in a frenzy and clobbered everything inside. When the source of the sound wasn't found, the demon moved down the hall.

The bed was overturned. The wall-mounted TV was smashed in, and based on the shape, Gabe imagined it was impaled by the creature's glowing skull. A Les Paul guitar lay on the ground, cord still plugged into a busted Line 6 amplifier, with a broken neck connected by the strings stretched like a homicide victim's guts. Clothes and blankets were strewn about, and books, movies, and video games littered the floor. Above, the ceiling fan was tilted on its side due to a crudely bent down rod.

The boys were surveying the symphony of destruction from the doorway when the hollow growl gravitated from the opposite end of the hall. Logan jumped into the room and made Gabe trip onto his back. His Raiders hat flew off and onto a torn Grand Theft Auto poster.

"Where'd it come from?" Gabe asked, sitting up and pushing Logan off him. He rubbed his rear end, the first thing to hit, and grabbed his hat.

Logan turned over and raised a shaky finger. "That way, I think."

Gabe stood and peeked into the hallway. It looked darker down there, like staring down the throat and into a beast's stomach. He gulped at the sight, then pushed himself forward out into the hall.

Behind, Logan slowly got to his feet and found his bat. He shivered and stepped out to meet Gabe. Seeing him jerking his eyes from side to side, Gabe thought of the other boys and wished *he* had the better batter with him.

"Be on guard," Gabe said to himself as much as to Logan. He felt his heartbeat in his throat. The stillness around him made him skittish, as if the creature would jump out of the shadows at any moment. The dark skin and skinny frame wouldn't be hard to hide in the dark, but the glowing skull would give it away. But what if it could turn off the light? He exhaled a deep breath he hadn't realized he was holding, and gooseflesh slithered up his arms.

*Christ*, he thought, *is not seeing the monster worse than staring it in the face?*

"Maybe if we can catch it by surprise," he said as they reached Rachel's door, "we'll have the upper hand."

"Yeah, right," Logan whispered, gripping his bat tightly. "The only way we'd have the upper hand is if it was hogtied and we all had bazookas."

Gabe closed his eyes and took another deep breath. He leaned over far enough to look inside.

"All clear!" he whispered back to Logan, who sighed with relief.

"I'm going in this time," Logan said, pushing past him.

"Hey!" Gabe whispered. "What—"

"It's my turn," Logan insisted with pursed his lips. "You stand guard this time."

With that he turned around and continued into the room, stepping slowly, looking high and low with his bat resting on his shoulder.

Gabe stood in the doorway, looking around the bedroom. Everything looked dead. The nail polish on Rachel's dresser was a rainbow of ashen grays. Her old softball jersey, once gold with navy letters, was now a washed-out black on a weathered bone white. The entire room was monochromatic and lifeless. His stomach hurt the longer he looked.

He turned his eyes away from the room and peered down the dark hallway. Two doors down,

French doors stood ajar. One of them was crooked, appearing unhinged and askew.

"Logan," Gabe said. "I think they're down this way."

"Hold up," said Logan, looking at the overturned dresser with spilled socks, bras, and various underwear. "I want to savor being in Rachel's room. Even if she's not here."

Gabe shook his head. "Even in hell, you're still a horndog."

Logan stopped leafing through grey and white panties and dropped his chin, biting the inside of his mouth.

"It helps keep my mind off all...this," he admitted with a soft sigh, gesturing to the world around him.

There was no way Logan got as much tail as he let on, Gabe thought. Even with his killer hairdo. It was a front or some sort of coping mechanism. They all had their way of dealing with their demons. Evan had his parents. James had baseball. Gabe had his thrash metal t-shirts and horror movies. What did Caleb have? He was the only normal kid of the bunch, or as normal as a rich kid could be. In a way, he was the only outsider because he was the only regular guy. He wasn't weird at all. Maybe Caleb's coping mechanism was the other kids. Caleb's motley crew of ragtag rascals.

And it was up to them to save him.

Gabe stepped out of Rachel's room.

"Where are you going?" Logan whispered harshly. "Stay here!"

"I'm going to check something out."

Gabe moved away and then poked his head back in. "If you hear a scream, run."

Logan gulped but nodded.

Gabe stepped softly down the hall, back to the wall and eyes searching for danger in the shadows. While reaching for the French doors, he made note of a linen closet across the hall in case he had to disappear quickly. He gripped the baseball in his hand and wiped cold sweat from his brow with the other before leaning forward to look through the crack between the doors.

It was the master suite. Like Caleb's room, it was torn asunder. It was hard to see, but he saw shadows moving in the room. His heart leaped for a moment, then dropped like a rock when he saw the dark hulking figure. It was looking in the opposite direction, pointing its shining light at something on the floor that Gabe couldn't see.

Gabe inched the doors open enough to see what the creature was looking at. There, on the floor, Caleb stared up at the monster, his eyes wide open with a frozen expression on his face.

Gabe pulled away from the door. His chest cinched with sadness, but his eyes couldn't look away. Caleb was dead. Or was he? His unblinking eyes were open, but he was stiff as a board. What was that thing doing to him?

"What are you looking at?" Logan whispered from behind him.

Gabe jumped back and felt his hair turn gray under his Raiders cap. Instinctively, he raised his hand with the baseball and almost bashed Logan's face in, but he stopped himself. He put a hand over Logan's mouth and put a finger to his lips.

Logan's eyebrows furrowed but he kept quiet. Silently, he moved his eyes to the doorway and peered inside. His eyes grew round, and he took a step back.

"What the fuck are we going to do?" He put his back against the wall.

Gabe looked away and bit his lip. That was the question, one he wasn't sure how to answer. Then he looked down in his hand at the baseball.

"Go tell the guys," he whispered to Logan. "I'm going to distract the monster so we can get Caleb out of there."

"What are you going to do?"

Gabe raised the ball and pointed to the end of the hall.

"Not yet!" Logan whispered his disapproval. "Wait until I get back!"

"Might be too late by then," Gabe reasoned. "Just get your big ass moving."

Logan stepped back with narrow eyes. "My ass isn't big," he said, then turned and jogged away.

Gabe watched until he disappeared down the stairs. He counted to five and raised his arm. He took a deep breath and threw the ball down the hall. By the time it landed with two thuds and a crash into the window decorations, he was already slipping into the linen closet and closing the door behind him. He shivered and quaked with towels pressed against his back and his nose bent by the door, closed off in complete darkness.

A loud hollow roar reverberated in the hallway followed by a loud crash of wood and thundering footsteps. Gabe squeezed his eyes shut and held his breath, bracing for an impact that never came. The sounds drummed down the hall and into the distance.

*Now or never,* he thought.

Gabe turned the knob and peeked into the hall. No sign of THE BEING. His heart was pounding in his ears, he dashed across the hall and through the now-opened doorway into the master suite.

Caleb lay lifeless on the ground beside a smashed TV. His eyes were open, but no life glowed behind them. Gabe stepped around a broken dresser and twisted bed sheets and dropped down to his knees.

"Caleb. Caleb!" He hesitated to touch him, but he grabbed his limp arm and hunted for a pulse at his wrist. "Come on, man. Don't be dead. Don't be dead!"

Gabe felt Caleb's neck. He couldn't feel a heartbeat no matter where he felt. He looked up to see if his chest was rising but tears clouded his vision.

Memories of his brother on the floor of his bedroom flooded his mind's eye. He had searched for a pulse, then, not finding it, had seized up. He was worthless then, and that same dull pain weighed on him now as his breaths came up short one after another.

He wiped away the tears blinding his eyes and grabbed Caleb's shoulders. His friend needed him to be strong. No more hiding behind his thrash metal t-shirts and horror films.

"Damnit, Caleb, wake up!" He shook the body a few times then slapped him across the face through gritted teeth. The sound of the clap scared Gabe as it broke the silence in the room, but from it came life.

Caleb's eyes closed and his face winced. He brought a hand up to his face and he let out a cry of pain. His eyes widened in horror as he looked about the room with frantic jerks, pushing Gabe away and gasping for breath.

Gabe grabbed him tight and pulled his friend into a hug. Caleb started to back off, pushing against him with his hands, but soon calmed down and returned the hug. His short breaths slowed, and he began to weep.

"Oh, god," he cried. "What a goddamn nightmare!"

"It's not over," Gabe said, "but I'm glad you're not toast just yet."

Caleb released his embrace and scooted back. Veins stuck out of his neck and panic returned to his face.

"We're not toast," he said, looking over Gabe's shoulder. "But we *are* fucked…"

Gabe opened his mouth to ask what he meant but shut it when he heard thumps and a low growl behind them. A glowing light drenched them, and Gabe saw the busted TV blink to life. He swiveled around and he knew they were dead.

# SIX

"Down the hall!" Logan yelled as he ran, leading the boys up the stairs and pointing down the hall. "That way!"

Evan tried to keep up. His chest burned and his legs felt rubbery, but he dared not stop. Earlier today, back in the real world, he couldn't imagine running toward danger in any capacity. Now, he was running toward it with a helmet rocking on his head, a football tucked under his arm, and a baseball in his hand.

He figured Caleb would do the same for him, but that wasn't why he went. It was his duty to protect his friend, and that gave him strength. He was part of a unit heading into battle. He couldn't let down his fellow soldiers.

They rounded the top banister and raced down the hall. Evan knew they looked ridiculous.

The three of them were in everyday clothes, socked feet, using sports equipment to chase down a monster. It was absurd, terrifying, and stupid, but it was the most badass Evan had ever felt.

"In here!" Logan took them across a pile of boards that looked to have once been doors and into a large bedroom. There, they halted. James bumped into Logan, who, in turn, was hit by Evan.

"Holy shit," Logan whispered. James looked up, shaking his head with a tight expression. Evan shook under his helmet, eyes looking all around, taking it all in.

Gabe and Caleb sat on the floor drenched in an eerie glow, wide eyes and mouths open in silent screams. They sat upright, but they looked dead and pale in the light. The demon towered above them, suspended on its skinny black limbs, directing its grinning, glowing skull at the two boys.

"Holy shit," Logan repeated.

James raised his bat to his shoulder. "We've got to save them!"

Evan surveyed the scene. Goosebumps traveled across his neck as his mind exploded with terror. The words Gabe said earlier floated back in his ears. Just shut your eyes and ride it out. But his eyes didn't cooperate. Inside, his stomach churned and knotted, but he was more compelled to help his friends than to save himself.

"Hey, dick-ass!" Evan heard his own voice blurt out. "Over here!"

Without a second thought, he raised the baseball in his hand, brought it back, and let it loose. It flew through the air in slow motion as the creature reared its bony mug. The baseball hit with minimal pressure, but the surprise was enough to make the creature jump and release a harrowing shriek of pain and fury. It redirected its attention to the boys in the doorway.

The large empty eye sockets widened. The jaw moved up and down, sizing them up as a lion might before it sinks its fangs into a dying gazelle. Finally, it opened its jaws wide and launched toward Evan's blood-drained face. The glowing was now as intense as a welder's spark and just as painful to the eyes, but Evan couldn't look away.

To his left, James stepped up to bat. In an instant, he aimed for the advancing skull and swung his bat through the air with a twist of his body and the drive of a locomotive. Evan always knew James was a powerful hitter, but now he got a first-hand demonstration of how hard he could smack the Louisville slugger. Pretty damn hard as it turned out.

The bat connected with the side of the demon's head, striking the bloody flesh around the skull with an audible THUNK. The demon let out a single stifled scream and tumbled onto the floor.

Behind the fallen creature, Gabe and Caleb jumped back to reality and rushed to meet the other boys.

THE BEING raised itself and turned around. The jaw worked up and down and side to side. It hesitated, and for a moment, it looked afraid of them. But the fearful look quickly disappeared as it reached a skeletal hand out towards the boys.

James squared up and swung again. This time, he aimed for the lanky hand reaching for him.

The hand clenched and retracted as the demon let out a wounded roar. The boys took this opportunity to escape.

"Get the hell out of here!" James shouted at Gabe and Caleb. They obliged, shielding their eyes from the glow as they exited the room. James and Logan raised their bats and started to back out of the room.

THE BEING let out an angry roar and raised its arms. The sound was so loud and shrill that it popped Evan's ears. He looked over his shoulder to see that down the hall Gabe and Caleb had started down the stairs. Now it was their turn.

"We've got to go!" he shouted.

James nodded and lunged forward for one last swing of his bat at one of the reaching hands. It dodged, and another of its hands grabbed the bat with its long fingers. THE BEING stared into James's eyes and momentarily paralyzed the all-star. It raised the bat and lifted James, who was still unconsciously gripping the bat, along with it. The glowing skull screamed, and the monster's hands snapped the bat in half like a toothpick.

James fell to the floor and wailed in pain. His hands still gripped the bat that was now severed just above the grip shaft. The monster grabbed Logan's bat but before he could be dragged with it, the boy let go and stumbled backward to escape the room. Now, the creature moved over James and the glow from its skull brightened as it released a rib rattling roar.

"James!" Evan yelled. His adrenaline was spiked, and his thoughts raced because of it. His helmet wobbled as he backed up, obstructing his view. Finally, all the pressure came to a head. He dropped the football and removed his helmet.

"Yo! Fuck dick!" He shouted, gripping the face guard like a handle. He hurled the helmet at the colossal creature with all his might.

To his delight, the helmet hit the skull with a loud CLUNK!

The beast was silenced immediately, and it shrank back in agony. Two of its hands covered its face and the others blindly swept the room for the boys, breaking and busting the furniture and walls. The boys took their chance to sprint down the hall and down the stairs.

THE BEING's roar sounded more and more distant as they slid down into the basement, but the drumming footsteps continued searching.

# SEVEN

"Holy shit," Evan said after they had rebuilt the barricade. He removed his glasses and wiped sweat from his brow. "We made it! I can't believe we made it!"

"Sure, we made it," Logan said. "But now what? How do we get home?"

"I don't know," James admitted, folding his arms, "but I'm glad I didn't have to stare into that thing's face too long."

He rubbed his arms as if he were cold and shared a knowing look with Caleb. The boys sat crowded around Gabe's phone, which sat face down on the ground with the flashlight shining up like an electric campfire.

"It made me see things," James said. "It was like a dream. I can't really remember it, but I felt...sad...and scared."

"It was a nightmare," Caleb said softly. He was sitting with his knees to his chest, a vacant look in his eyes. "I was running through the school trying to find a way out, but all the exits were bricked up. Every room I entered..."

He stopped, looked up at each of them then lowered his eyes and continued.

"It was like *Hellraiser*, you know, the one with the hooks. I saw my mom, dad, Rachel, and all of you guys in different rooms being...tortured. You all had hooks pulling your skin and your bodies were burning. God, I can still smell it."

He shuddered and held his hand in front of his face, scrunching his nose.

"It was horrible. It replayed over and over until Gabe shook me awake."

James reached over and put a hand on his shoulder but gazed away, lost in his own thoughts. Gabe stared down with his arms folded. He was doing his best to keep from crying as he remembered his own nightmare.

"What did you see, Gabe?" He heard Evan ask softly from across the room.

Gabe looked up, swallowed, and shook his head. His shoulders slumped in a withdrawn way.

"My brother..." he started to say, then stopped as the images stirred again.


He had awakened, standing in the doorway to the black-and-white auditorium where the experiment had happened in the movie. The cold air from the room drew goosebumps to his arms and down his back. Across a sea of thrown folding chairs, the wall was bare. The portal was gone. Gabe could smell cigarette smoke, but there was something far worse lingering underneath. It made him gag, and he covered his nose and mouth with his palm. He couldn't identify it in the moment, but Caleb was right on the money: burnt flesh. The floor was littered with motionless bodies, scorched from electric shock. They were lacerated and bloody.

Gabe turned away from the auditorium and moved down a high windowed hall. Outside the glass, a storm-like fire rolled overhead, and the same ashy snow fell. A peek outside showed him another barren desert. He was on yet another lonely island in hell.

The light in the windows began to darken. Large, dark, skeletal legs stepped past the window. Gabe shivered, frozen in fear, unable to run or scream as limbs the size of tree trunks shook the ground with each thundering step. They stopped when they shadowed him in the hall, and he gasped sharply as a large glowing skull dropped into view of the window. It was the demon, except it was now more than twice the size of the one that stepped through the screen.

Gabe broke into a sprint down the hall. Outside, the thundering steps began going again, charging up slowly and growing louder until it sounded like an oncoming freight train. Gabe's legs couldn't sprint fast enough. Double doors at the end of the hall moved further and further away the more he advanced. The glowing death approached behind him. He found another set of double doors off to the side and charged against them, shoulder first.

Now, he was in the basement.

The theater was dark, and the seating was torn and flipped over. The walls were littered with scratch marks and the sports bar was smashed in. The projector swung, attached only by wires from the ceiling, flashing the only light in the room onto the floor. Gabe's heart thrashed in his chest and tinged with sharp pain as he saw four bodies in the light. Four bodies, bloodied and slashed in a macabre massacre.

Gabe wept and stumbled back out of the doorway. Outside in the hall, the beast was gone from the window. He tried to catch his breath until he realized he was holding something in his clenched fists. Two hatchets, each drenched and dripping with black blood.

He screamed and threw them to the floor. They landed with loud clangs and bounced in large dark puddles on the floor. Gabe stepped back away from them with a gripping scream, only to slip on the blood and onto his back in the pool. He scooted back, trying to get out of the puddle, but he found himself slipping to the ground again and again, becoming increasingly covered and sticky with blood.

Finally, he closed his eyes and put his hands to his face, screaming with all the force he could muster. When he opened his eyes, the blood was gone. He sat on the floor in the white hall as clean as he had entered.

He was alone.

Gabe sat in a fetal position with his head between his knees and wept loudly. Snot fell with the tears and spit dribbled down his chin. For several minutes, all he could do was cry, shivering and shaking on the floor. But soon, he heard the sound of galloping steps behind him down the dark hallway. This time, they did not come from outside.

THE BEING stepped from a shadow in the dark hallway. The skull was not glowing, as if it had turned it off to hide. Its larger frame filled the hallway, and the skull screamed as the creature dug its large, bony hands into the walls and floor. It charged.

Gabe jumped to his feet and ran without wiping his face. He could hardly see through his tears, but he threw his arms and legs into overdrive without a second thought. His lungs ached as he drew shallow breath after shallow breath to keep himself moving. The hallway before him stood still this time and he approached the end at a rapid pace, slamming into another set of double doors.

Inside, he fell to his hands and knees onto familiar shaggy gray carpet. The smells of old socks and cologne filled his nostrils. He raised his head and saw posters of *The Evil Dead*, *My Bloody Valentine*, and *Megadeth* on the walls, still in the monochromatic filter. He was in his brother's room. He turned around to see if THE BEING had followed, but instead of the double doors to the hallway, he saw a long-haired teenager leaning over a body.

Gabe got to his feet and felt the blood drain from his face. His lips quivered as he stepped forward. The smell of scorched skin filled the air and he halted mid-step. He could hear chewing and the ripping and grinding of slimy fibers between teeth.

He started to turn away, but then he caught a glimpse of the body. It, too, had long hair but also had a thick, patchy beard. Immediately, Gabe knew it was his brother. He walked next to the teenager and looked over his shoulder. His brother stared up from the floor, lifeless, with empty eye sockets, limbs spread out on the floor. In his mouth was a lightbulb, the cap wedged between his teeth. His chest had been split wide open, displaying blackened gore and serrated bones. Around the edges of the gaping wound were bite marks with ripped and torn fleshy bits hanging by threads.

Gabe gasped. His tears fell once again and he began to hyperventilate with short, stabbing pains in his chest.

*I'm going to be sick! I'm going to be sick!*

He pulled his body back, but his feet were planted and unmoving. He gripped his face tight to keep the scent of death out of his nostrils.

The teenager bent over once again, reached inside the bleeding cavity, and scraped into the flesh with his fingers. Dark fluid oozed onto the floor. Protruding rib bones moved about as the hands fished around inside. Finally, the hands retracted from the crevasse, fists gripping wads of bleeding meat, and the teenager brought them to his mouth. Gabe stared at him as he chewed. His own face turned to stare back and slowly smiled with dark blood dripping from his lips and chin, chunks of meat stuck between his teeth.

His brother's head shot up from the floor, his empty eyes staring up at him. Gabe screamed, and then he immediately began choking. He leaned over and coughed up spongy hunks from his throat. When they fell to the ground, he saw they were wads of chewed meat and small, white, partially dissolved pills. His face and hands were slick with blood. He looked around for the feasting teenager, but he was gone. He realized it had been himself! He dropped to his knees again, wailing with tears streaming down his bloody cheeks, and began to dry heave.

Behind him, a bright glow drenched him, and the hairs stood on the back of his neck. He turned his head. The giant glowing skull grinned down at him as it slowly swooped towards him, opening its mouth as it approached.

Gabe turned away so as to not look in the light. Gabe raised a hand to shield against the intense brightness. The lightbulb in his brother's mouth shined brightly as his brother worked around the bulb and then chomped his teeth down, shattering the glass with his teeth. He began chewing the broken glass with horrifying crunches. Then he opened his mouth and gave a sinister smile. Shards of glass stuck in his gums and black ooze dripped from his mouth and down his chin.

Then, his brother spoke in a deep, distorted voice, "Terror reigns!"

Gabe woke to find his friends alive, ready to fight the monster in the bedroom. He hadn't had time to process what nightmare he'd had until now. As he sat with the others, he began to weep again and feel the familiar sharp pains in his heart.

"Doesn't matter," he said through slowing cries. "We just need to figure out a way out of here."

Gabe wiped his eyes and looked up at the group. It was Caleb's turn to comfort. He reached an arm around his cousin and gripped him tight. Gabe returned with a big squeeze then cleared his throat and composed himself.

"I think I have an idea," Gabe said. "In the kitchen, I saw something weird, but I didn't really think about it until I saw it again upstairs."

Caleb narrowed his eyes at Gabe and Evan shifted in place. James leaned in while Logan stared at the wall.

"When the glow from the skull went over the fridge, I could've sworn I heard the fridge click on and start humming," Gabe said. "When the glow moved away, it stopped."

Gabe looked at his friends, all of whom were listening intently.

"It happened again upstairs," he continued. "The TV on the floor in Caleb's parents' room clicked on for a second when that thing shined its light on us. It was busted, but the screen turned on anyway. And when we ran away back to the basement the first time after James thew the doorstop, did you guys hear anything?"

James nodded and said, "There was some static feedback. Sounded like a screech. I don't know what it was."

"I'm pretty sure it was Caleb's guitar and amp," Gabe said. "The monster's light could have turned it on when it went upstairs after the door-stop."

"When I was in the light," Evan said excitedly, "I felt little hairs stand up on my arm! My neck, too. And it felt like when we went to the Discovery Center as a kid and touched that big lightning ball."

"Mine too!" Gabe said with a grin.

"Static electricity," Logan pursed his lips and nodded. "So what?"

"When it got mad," Gabe said, "the light got brighter. Maybe it can power more when it gets excited."

"So what if it could? What's that to us?" Logan's voice was rising as he spoke. "It won't fix the damn projector!"

Logan pointed up to the dead projector and the boys' gaze followed.

"Maybe it can," Gabe said. "I might have an idea, but we'd need to lure him down here."

"Are you *trying* to kill us?" Logan asked exasperated. "Let's just hold off for a while and see what happens."

"Do you think someone's coming to save us?" Caleb asked. His face was shadowy and dark, his tone angry. It was one of the few times Gabe had seen his cousin with an angry expression, and it made him look away.

"This is its home," Caleb continued. "This is *its* world, and *we* are the strangers here. You said the only thing outside is a fucking desert of ash and a fiery storm, so where are we going to go?"

Logan frowned and folded his arms. He started to say something but was interrupted by a series of steps from above. The boys looked up. James gripped his broken bat. Logan hunched his shoulders and fixed his hair. Evan didn't move an inch but stared up with round eyes. Caleb was the only one looking down, shielding his eyes as if sitting in the sun.

Gabe's eyes returned to the ceiling, following the steps as best he could. Soon, he couldn't distinguish the sound of the steps from the thumping in his chest, but he knew right where the beast was headed. He looked at the door at the top of the stairs, the barricade of chairs was a shadowy bush in the dark. To his horror, a light spilled in through the bottom of the door. He sucked in a deep breath so fast he thought he would choke, but he dared not move or cough. The light intensified, becoming brighter as footsteps thumped outside. After a few seconds, the light moved away with the footsteps.

"We can't stay here," Caleb whispered, tears swelling in his eyes. "If Gabe has a plan, we should try it. We can't keep sitting here waiting for it to find us."

"He's right," Gabe looked up then cleared his throat. "We should try to get out of here, even if it's a long shot."

He paused for a moment and looked at the boys, making sure their eyes met his, then pointed at the projector.

"We came here from some sort of portal. As long as the projector's out, we're stuck. The light from the monster's face seems to power electronics. Maybe if we can get it down here, we can get the projector portal powered back up."

"Like *Back to the Future*?" James chuckled to himself. He was lightly touching the splinters at the end of the broken bat in his hands. "The lightning bolt gives the car enough electricity to power the time machine."

"Exactly!" Gabe smiled.

"Okay," Logan sighed with his arms still folded. "But even if we get him down here and make him stare at the projector, what happens then? Do we just jump through the screen?"

Gabe shrugged. "I don't know. Maybe. I think we'll know what to do when it happens."

"Great," Logan said, slapping his knees. "So, we'll just lure the bastard down here to open a portal or something—maybe it'll fire up the popcorn maker too—and hope that somehow we find a way out of this nightmare before it rips us apart?"

Gabe looked at Caleb. They both said nothing.

"Jesus," Logan scoffed and shook his head. "That *is* the plan."

"We beat its ass before," James said quietly, still examining the broken bat as if he lost a dear friend. "We can do it again."

Caleb nodded. "At least long enough to see if we can escape."

James stared dreamily at the splintered bat. "I bet that fucker still has the Cardinals logo on its face."

"Isn't it crazy?" Evan said, removing his glasses and wiping the lenses on his shirt. "I mean, we can go through the screen. That's nuts."

"All of this is fucking crazy," Caleb said, raising his eyebrows and tilting his head.

"It's how we got here," Gabe said. "It might be our only way out."

Logan put his elbows on his knees, leaned forward, and sighed. He had taken his phone out of his pocket and rubbed it between his fingers. Though it was dead, it seemed to comfort him.

"Okay," he said. "How do we get him down here?"

"One of us will have to get its attention, call for him, then lure him to the projector," James said, leaning forward.

"So, we play cowboy and corral a monster," Logan said, rolling his eyes. "Great! But how do we keep him from following us through the portal?"

"What about a Molotov cocktail?" Caleb asked. He threw a thumb over his shoulder in the direction of the bar. "We could use the liquor bottles over there. There are lighters in one of the drawers. We could throw it and burn the bastard while we make the escape."

"Hell yeah!" James stood up with a grin on his face. "I've always wanted to throw a Molotov."

Gabe felt a smile cross his face and a jolt of energy surge through him.

"Alright," he said, getting to his feet. "Let's get the fucker!"

Gabe held the light as the boys searched the bar for materials. James grabbed a bottle of booze and held it up to the light. Liquid sloshed up into the neck like an angry sea. It was a bottle of Jameson.

"Let's do this one," he laughed. "It's got my name on it."

Behind him, Caleb and Logan rummaged through the kitchen drawers for the next items. Logan found a lighter shaped like a long metal wand with a trigger. Caleb grabbed a rag, ripped it in half, and stuffed it down the Jameson bottle's throat. After tipping it upside down and shaking it a few times, it soaked up the whiskey and became a smelly wick for their explosive candle.

Gabe looked at the others. "Are we ready?" he asked.

Caleb nodded with the confident smile of a loyal friend. James stood with a hand on his hip and the other on the grip of his splintered bat. It was his hero stance, the pinnacle of the all-American boy with his baseball cap and driven gaze. Beside him stood Logan with his head cocked to one side, arms folded, his hair perfect. Evan stared back at Gabe with no sign of fear on his face. Instead, his eyes were narrow and intense, like that of an adventurer about to start an expedition.

"We're ready," Evan said.

Gabe nodded and smiled, "Let's do this."

# EIGHT

After a few rounds of Rock Paper Scissors, Gabe lost the tournament and was crowned "live bait." Otherwise, he wouldn't have walked upstairs by himself for any reason.

After moving the barricade of chairs enough to slide out, he turned to look back downstairs at his crew. They stared back. Caleb gave two thumbs up, and Gabe gave him the finger.

He drew a deep breath and then reached for the knob. It turned easily, and the door swung open enough for him to slip through. From the hall, he could hear slow thumps from the creeping creature as it went about on its hunt for the boys. Gabe took a deep breath and slid into the hall.

Just got to call the monster, then book it back, he thought as he pushed his back against the wall.

He looked both ways, neither seeing nor hearing anything now. The hallway had gone quiet. Where had the last thump come from? Upstairs? He stepped farther out into the hallway, cleared the fear from his throat, and turned toward the stairs. It was time to shine.

He took another deep breath and shouted, "Hey, you ugly bag of dicks!" He cupped his hands around his mouth and yelled, "Come down here before I give your mom's phone number to Logan!"

Nothing. No thumps thundering his way. No angry roars. Only silence, which was always somehow worse. How did he lose a colossal monster?

"He's going to send her pictures of his baby carrot!" someone yelled from downstairs.

Despite his fear, Gabe chuckled. He turned to yell at his friends when he found himself drenched in light. The hairs on his neck rose and his balls pulled up into his throat. He looked around but didn't see the monster. He raised his hand to shield himself against the glow, which he now realized was coming from the ceiling. Above him, he saw only darkness and a large glowing skull grinning down at him.

It had turned off its glow to hide in the shadows! Just like his dream!

The light intensified as the skull's mouth opened wide. It uncoiled its body and released its claws from the ceiling. It roared, preparing to lunge at its prey.

"Holy shit!" Gabe slipped back downstairs. The demon rammed the doorway. Its skull reached through, but its shoulders caught the doorframe. The stairs were now lighted by the demonic glow and the boys got a good view of Gabe as he tumbled down the stairs. The creature screamed from above and rammed the doorway again.

"That was fast!" Caleb yelled over the banging, giving Gabe a hand to his feet.

"The fucker's slippery," he said with a hand on his chest. "He was camping just outside the door. It knew where we were. It's smarter than we thought."

"Hopefully we're smarter. Come on!"

Above them, the monster crashed into the doorway one last time, and an avalanche of monochromatic material exploded down the stairs. It emerged through the cloud of destruction with the speed of a charging predator. Its arms ripped the walls away and broke through the railing.

THE BEING leapt from the collapsing stairway and landed on the floor at the base of the stairs. It gazed at the boys from hollow sockets as it rose up in one slow movement.

"Is it bigger?" Evan yelled in a shrill voice. "It looks *bigger*!"

Gabe didn't answer. His heart was racing in his ears and his eyes stared unblinking at the monstrosity.

"Steady!" Caleb yelled at the boys. "Back it up to the projector!"

They ran to the front row of the theater and the demon's glow followed them, watching as they backed themselves into the far corner.

THE BEING approached and once its glow illuminated the projector, the screen lit up. The boys were drenched in bright light and the portal appeared behind them. Gabe found himself smiling at the sight. He was so happy he nearly forgot the danger.

Nearly.

"James!" Caleb yelled. "Now!"

James lit the Jameson Molotov's wick and sent it sailing through the air.

THE BEING lunged toward the seats with a fierce roar, all four arms stretched out reaching for the boys. It opened its jaws wide and the bottle smashed against its skull-like face. Its charging body froze mid-step. A brief roar escaped its mouth, then transformed into high-pitched bursts of distorted static. Sparks traveled across the skull. The jaw popped out of place, and the whole head tilted sideways, like a snarling dog suddenly wondering where the ball went. Where the Molotov landed, a small puddle of flames gently licked a few inches off the ground.

"Get through the portal!" Caleb screamed, pointing to the wall behind him.

James led the way and rushed to the wall with his shoulder. Just before contact, the light went dim, and he slammed into the wall. The other boys sandwiched him against the wall before collapsing in a dogpile.

"Fuck!" Logan yelled, pushing Evan off him. "Now what?"

Gabe got to his feet and looked at the projector. It was still on but the light was dim. The skull's light had turned away when it began glitching and the power to the projector had diminished. It staggered away, shaking its skull.

"What a dud!" James said, pointing to the broken glass on the floor.

"If we don't turn it back to the projector," Gabe yelled to Caleb, "we're not going anywhere!"

Caleb nodded and got to his feet.

"Let's get that bastard back here!"

THE BEING stopped glitching and turned back toward the boys. Its teeth ground in anger. It lowered itself and charged them. The glow of the skull drenched them in bright light as it closed in, the projector brightened once again, but the predator was charging too fast.

"Oh, shit!" Gabe yelled. "Run!"

Gabe pushed Evan off to the left side with James running close behind after grabbing his splintered bat. Caleb and Logan dove out of the way just in time to escape the charge. The beast slammed into the theater seats, narrowly missing the boys with its grasping skeletal hands.

The boys ran their separate ways but met behind the sports bar. Logan's fingers clasped his hair, and his eyes darted back and forth.

"Fuck, fuck, fuck!" he screamed. "We're so fucked! Now what do we do?"

"We fight back!" Caleb screamed back at him, a vein pulsing in his forehead. He pulled a steak knife out of the silverware drawer and a bottle of Jack Daniels from the liquor shelf. James grabbed a baseball from a shelf behind the counter and hurled it at the beast. The ball knocked the side of its head. It stopped for a moment but then lunged full force at the bar.

Logan screamed and ran. Gabe followed, hearing Evan's heavy breaths behind him. Before they could run back to the theater, the creature jumped in front of them, cornering them between the bar and the broken staircase.

Caleb hurled the bottle of Jack at the demon's head. It connected with a *CLINK* and shattered onto the floor in a puddle of dark liquid and broken glass. The creature roared with abysmal rage as its arms reached out to seize them. One bony hand grabbed James, another grabbed Caleb. Two more snatched Gabe and Logan with long fingers, clenching them with tremendous strength. They struggled and shouted in vain. THE BEING lifted Gabe to its skull. He winced and squeezed his eyes shut.

One of Caleb's arms was spared from the demon's grasp. He raised the steak knife over his head and brought it down into its hand. The shiny blade disappeared as it punctured the beast's dark skin, sinking to the handle. Black blood flowed from the wound and the beast reared back and screeched in agony. THE BEING released Caleb from its grasp and flung him across the room.

To Gabe's relief, the beast released him as well, but he landed on the busted Jack Daniels bottle, and the broken glass sliced his skin. Blood flowed down his leg in a gushing black line. He grasped his left leg with a grimace and crawled out of the way.

Above him, James and Logan were still in the beast's clutches. The fingers kept them strapped into the unhinged roller coaster as it swung them left and right, still reeling from its bleeding hand. Logan beat his fists against the hand that bound him. The grips were growing tighter in the monster's agony.

With the broken bat still in hand, James aimed and stabbed the splintered end into the demon's wrist and then twisted it like a key. When he pulled back on the bat, the screaming skull shrieked and dropped the boys to the floor, its other hands moving to protect its bleeding wrist.

The boys landed hard and with cries of pain, but James hopped up and took advantage of the opportunity to really put the hurt on THE BEING. He ran under its hulking mass and stabbed the broken bat upward into its gut. James twisted the splintered stump and black blood flooded from the piercing. While THE BEING seized in pain, the boys ran to the projector.

Evan was first to arrive in the projector light followed by James and Logan. Gabe was still struggling to his feet and gritting his teeth in pain. His leg was a dripping mess of black blood. He turned to see how close the creature was, but instead saw Caleb pull his arm over his shoulder and then help him up. Before he could say anything, Evan slid under his other arm and helped him move along. He looked down at the short, pudgy boy in glasses and grimaced; it was as close to a smile as he could get. Together, they rushed to the projector screen.

With a loud hollow roar, the beast reared its head and galloped toward them with rumbling steps. Once the glow of its skull touched the projector, the portal became bright and opened once again.

"Go, go, go!" Caleb pushed the others. "Now's our chance!"

Without a moment's thought, James and Logan jumped into the screen. They disappeared as if slipping behind a curtain shining as bright as the sun.

"Go, Caleb!" Evan cried with a push.

Caleb threw him a surprised look but obliged. He turned and jumped into the portal, vanishing into the light.

Now, it was Gabe and Evan's turn. They leaned forward to jump when the light suddenly became dim once again.

"Oh, shit balls!" Evan yelled, pounding his fists against the screen.

They turned to see the beast circling around the seats to attack from the side. Its glowing skull grinned at them in the dark. The projector was no longer in the light and their portal was locked.

"Move your ass!" Gabe yelled. Evan got under Gabe's arm, and they booked it out of the theater area. The beast charged behind them with a bone-rattling howl. It knocked the leather recliners over and stabbed its bony fingers into the cushions.

"Fuck! Dick! Balls! Shit!" Evan screamed as they hobbled away like entries in a three-legged race. "Balls! Suck! Fuck! Dick!"

They passed the popcorn maker on their way to the bar. The beast grabbed the popcorn cart and flipped it over with a clanging, metal crash. The boys were surprised to make it to the bar alive, but their optimism dipped when they looked back.

The oil drum spilled when the popcorn maker tipped over. It must've been quite full because, when it combined with the flaming Jameson Molotov rags on the ground, it ignited into a fire that quickly spread across the carpet. The creature wailed as the flames blew in its face. It screeched and began blindly attacking the fire, destroying the basement in the process.

The boys ducked down behind the bar. Gabe hissed and winced as the pain in his leg sent shockwaves through his body. Evan slumped down next to him against the cabinet. Only now that they were hidden did Gabe see fear return to Evan's face. His glasses were smudged and sweat dripped down his forehead, wetting the tips of his bangs. He was a mess.

"I just wanted to play Fortnite!" He let his head bang back against the cabinet.

Gabe didn't respond. His leg was cut in several places. He ran his hand over the cuts. No glass, thank God, but he was bleeding like a spigot. His hand came back sticky and black.

"Shit!" he shook his head. "I'm a goddamn mess."

Evan raised his glasses and rubbed his face. "Why did the popcorn maker explode?" he asked.

"The cooking oil," Gabe said, wiping the sticky blood on his shirt. "There was a jug of it on the cart and I guess it's flammable."

"Okay," Evan said, wiping his brow, "but why didn't the Molotov explode?"

Gabe shrugged and closed his eyes. Why the hell was Evan asking these questions now? They could be crushed or petrified by the beast at any moment.

"I don't know, man!" he barked at Evan, unable to hold back his frustration any longer. "I guess there's more water in whiskey than we thought. So what?"

"Is that why the skull got shocked?"

Gabe opened his eyes. That was it!

"Yes! It stopped him in his tracks. That bastard must be electric. Maybe its glowing powers come from electricity or something. Like a lightbulb!"

He raised up on his good leg and began searching around the bar.

"If we could shock him again, that could stop him long enough to escape!"

"How are we going to do that? Throw another bottle at him?"

Gabe shrugged. "That's our best shot, but it's got to be something with a lot of water."

"What about this?" Evan held up a bottle of clear liquid.

"That's vodka," Gabe said, reading Tito's from the label. "It might work, but let's get out of here first. We're sitting ducks!"

Outside the bar counter, the sound of crackling fire and crumbling walls echoed around them. Then the beast growled, and its footsteps thumped in their direction.

They hunkered down behind the counter and crawled quickly around as the beast reached the counter. Its light doused the bar in light and the monster stared down the alley between the counter and the cabinets. The skull screamed and the creature reached for them, narrowly missing Gabe's limping leg.

Evan slid under Gabe's arm again and they staggered as fast as they could to the theater. The floor and walls were on fire, and the ceiling was crumbling down. Large chunks slanted down like ramps, exposing rooms and furniture above. Flames were beginning to climb upstairs and the basement was getting hotter than hell.

"We've got to get out of here!" Gabe yelled.

When they reached the screen, the projector light was totally gone. Gabe's heart dropped, but then he saw the dim image of the portal on the floor. He looked up at the projector. In the commotion, the demon had knocked it off the ceiling mount. It hung by a few cables and swung in a slow circle, casting the portal onto the floor. Gabe shuddered as he remembered his nightmarish trance.

"Let's make this quick before the projector disconnects!" Gabe said.

Evan nodded and looked at the vodka bottle in his hand.

"I sure wish James were here."

"Well, he's not," Gabe said, groaning through the pain in his leg. "And I can't throw worth a shit. It's all up to you."

THE BEING stepped through the fire. The heat throbbed on Gabe's face and sweat dripped at his temples. The skull's light intensified as the monster hunched to look the boys in the eye. With a devilish grin, it screamed and launched toward them in midair. When the glow touched the projector, it surged with power and the portal shined brightly onto the floor. Dark skeletal hands reached for the boys and Gabe held his breath.

"Suck this!" Evan said as he threw the bottle of vodka. Gabe worried he hadn't thrown it hard enough, but the bottle shattered on its face. At once, the demon began to glitch.

The skull seized, and the entire basement seemed to spasm along with it. The monster inched forward through the air with each seizing tremor as though jumping forward slowly through time. The crumbling ceiling rubble lagged on its way down. The flames flashed on and off. The portal switched from dim to bright as it swung on the cables like a pendulum. Their exit would have to be timed right.

"When do we jump? When do we jump?" Evan yelled over the jolting noises around them.

Gabe shook his head. His wide eyes couldn't blink, couldn't comprehend what was happening. He clenched his jaw, partially from the pain and partially from the terror inside him. By now, he could barely keep his good leg up. It throbbed in pain. He was tired. So very tired. If only his friends were here. If only his brother were here. What would he say?

Finally, he blinked as the idea came to him.

"Just close your eyes and jump!"

Evan adjusted his glasses and shot him a bewildered look.

"What the hell —"

"Trust me," Gabe said with a smile. "Just shut your eyes, jump, and ride it out."

Evan started to say something but then swallowed and nodded.

"Okay!"

They watched the portal swing back and forth, and then they closed their eyes and jumped. THE BEING was lunging through the air, seizing, and reaching for them. A hollow roar broke out around them, then distorted along with the sound of flames and the crashing of the world beyond.

# NINE

Evan opened his eyes. His mind was reeling, trying to comprehend what happened and where he was. Most importantly, did they make it? He pushed his stinging eyes open to see the dark basement.

He sat up and adjusted his glasses, thankful to feel the soreness in his body. He looked around, happy to notice three other things: the color of his skin was no longer ashy, the projector screen displayed silent static, and he smelled the greasy garlic of Domino's pizza.

In the projector light, he saw the other boys lying on the floor and the theater seats in a jumbled mess. At first, he thought they were dead, killed on impact, but was relieved to see their rising chests and hear their murmuring groans.

They made it.

They were out.

The basement was no longer crumbling. There were no flames. The room was silent. The beast was...

He gasped and looked around with jolting movements.

There was no sign of it. He sighed and got to his feet with wobbly legs, looked at the projector, and then stopped cold in his tracks. A shadow rose from below, reaching long arms upward toward the projector! The screen went dead, and the room went dark.

Moments later, the lights flicked on.

James stood by the light switch beside the screen. He had a hesitant but friendly smile on his face. Caleb was climbing down from the back row seats, taking deep breaths to slow his excited breathing. Above him, the power cable to the projector dangled loosely.

Logan uncoiled himself from a contorted shape on his seat. Evan looked around but didn't see Gabe.

"Guys!" he said, heart racing. "Where's Gabe?"

Caleb's eyebrows raised in alarm, and he hopped down.

"Down here..." a small voice from the second row called.

Gabe lay on the floor examining his leg. Cuts and dried blood marred his right leg, and smears of red painted his Exodus t-shirt. Caleb helped him up into a recliner.

"Holy shit," Logan said, furiously combing fingers through his hair. "So, it happened? We actually...went there?"

"It sure as shit wasn't a dream," Gabe said, pointing to his leg.

"Got that right," James said, raising a hand. A dark red liquid dripped down his hand and forearm. Evan winced, remembering James stabbing THE BEING in the gut.

"How's your leg?" Caleb asked Gabe.

"Sore," he said, "but the bleeding stopped. It'll need to be cleaned up, but the cuts aren't that deep. I'll probably have some gnarly scars, maybe a few—"

He was cut off by a loud BANG as the basement door flew open and footsteps headed down. Evan flinched at the sound.

"Caleb!" Rachel's strained voice made them all look toward the stairs. Her tired eyes narrowed, and her nostrils flared. "What the hell do you and your friends want? They said you were missing or something."

Caleb turned to the other boys with his mouth agape then turned back to his sister. Gabe slid down in his seat, hiding his bloody shirt from her.

"Um...sorry," was the best he could muster.

"Well, the house isn't burning down. No one's missing. So, why the hell am I here?"

No one said anything. Then, Logan piped up. "We-we watched a movie," he said like someone admitting murder.

Rachel dropped her chin with a half-lidded expression.

"You watched a movie?" she said. "So what?"

Logan looked at the others. No one said anything until Evan spoke up.

"It was scary," he said with a smile. "He wet his pants."

Logan dropped his jaw. "The hell I did!"

"You guys are so dumb," Rachel said and started up the stairs. She turned around on the second step and said, "Grow a pair, you scaredy-cats!"

They watched her ascend the stairs and exit the basement, slamming the door behind her.

Logan shook his head and turned to Evan with a grin.

"You son of a bitch!"

James leaned over to Evan with a smirk and offered his dripping red knuckles.

"Nice one, slugger."

Evan hesitated but bumped fists with James. It left a smear of red, but he didn't care.

James looked down at his hands.

"Oops. Sorry, Ev. Guess I should wash my hands and get this crap off me."

"Someone hand me my laptop," Gabe said. "I'm going to wipe it."

"Let's burn the damn thing," Caleb laughed. "After I get some pizza. I'm starving."

"Yeah," James agreed, following him to the bar. "It feels like we were gone longer than we were."

Logan pulled out his phone and followed them. Evan's stomach was finally relaxing, and he decided he needed a break, too. He went to his bag, retrieved his Switch, and plopped down next to Gabe in the seats.

"Thanks for saving my neck back there," Gabe said. "You really kicked some ass!"

Evan shrugged.

"I didn't have much of a choice. We were screwed anyway. I'm just glad I can finally relax and play some Fortnite."

Gabe nodded and pulled out his phone. Evan connected his Switch to Caleb's Wi-Fi. Fortnite had an update, so he watched the progress bar fill up, but before it was finished, he noticed that something else had begun installing. His mouth dropped open and froze, staring at the screen with widening eyes. The twists in his stomach began to wrench him once again.

On his home screen, a new game icon appeared next to Fortnite.

"Guys," he blurted out. "GUYS!"

"What the hell's the matter, man?" Gabe leaned over his shoulder and then dropped his jaw. "Oh, shit. Guys! Come here. Now!"

"Calm down, bro," James said. "What gives?"

They huddled around his chair and stared at his Switch screen. Staring up at them was THE BE-ING's frozen screaming skull, the icon for Evan's new game.

*Terror Zone!*

# Heroes of Terror Zone

This novella came to life thanks to the incredible support of my Kickstarter backers, friends, and family. Your contributions and encouragement helped give this story a killer debut.

Thank you for joining me on this adventure through Terror Zone!

| | |
|---|---|
| Adam Selby-Martin | Jireh |
| Adgee Harville | Karen Rogers |
| Andrew Kaplan | Kristopher Covey |
| Aron Gunnerson | Lori Polansky |
| Brennan Wolf | Matthew Fox |
| Chase Hampton | Sam Greening |
| Curtis Rowden | Shawn Latimer |
| Danielle Stewart | Stephen Fox |
| Dmytro Kocherhan | Steve Pattee |
| Drew Thompson | Thayne Mitchell |
| Ethan Anderson | Tyler Hulsey |
| Gilbert Perez | Walker Neer |
| James Powell | Zack Fissel |
| Jesy 🖤 | |

## About the Author

After becoming obsessed with Scooby-Doo at a young age, Vince Rogers began creating his own stories. His love for horror movies and books soon followed, sparking endless daydreams of monsters, ghouls, and things lurking in the stillness of the shadows.

Vince is currently working on new releases and continuing to chase the creatures in his attic. He lives in Ozark, Missouri, with his wife, Destiny, their two kids, and a condescending black cat.